Entopia

Written by
Kevin Noel Olson

Illustrations by
Jamison Challeen

Entopia
by Kevin Noel Olson

A Cornerstone Book
Published by Cornerstone Book Publishers
Story Copyright © 2007 by Kevin Noel Olson
Illustrations Copyright © 2007 by Jamison Calleen

Cornerstone Book Publishers
New Orleans, LA

First Cornerstone Edition - 2007

www.cornerstonepublishers.com

ISBN: 1-61342-225-3
ISBN-13: 978-1-61342-225-0

MADE IN THE USA

Dedication

For Nathan, Jaxie, Kimmie, Wesley, Emily, Cassidy, Aaron, Adam, Kaden, Daniel, Olivia, Sam, Caramia, Vincent, Hanna, Rebecca, Isaac, and all my younger friends and family. You are all the citizens of tomorrow, and the future looks bright because of you. I wish you the best as you continue your adventure in the world.

The book was really funny and surprising and sometimes it was kinda sad. When the spider, stinkbug, and scorpion protected the others so they could escape the rabbit hole I thought they were gone forever. I liked it when William Bee thought he was going to get eaten in the web. I liked all the insects and I liked Gordon the scorpion the best. William was nice when he said Gordon wasn't frightening. I liked reading the book a lot-it was a lot of fun.

CARAMIA - age 9

Table of Contents

Entopia

CHAPTER 1

William, like any young bee, loved to pollinate flowers. Yesterday, he saw some beautiful forget-me-nots sitting inside a large building, but a closed window stopped him from visiting them.

William lived in a nice beehive with his parents and his little brother Robert. William's mother had told him to stay out of buildings and to visit only the fields and gardens near the beehive where there were plenty of flowers. William usually listened to his mother, although he often strayed far from the beehive in his explorations. He remembered what his mom had said about staying out of buildings, but forget-me-nots didn't grow just anywhere and he'd never pollinated one. He really, really, REALLY wanted to play in the forget-me-nots!

William went by where he had seen the flowers. To his delight, he felt the cool air rush from the window as he flew past. 'The window is open!' William thought. He turned around and flew through the open window and right into the room. Judging by the pair of desks covered with papers and various objects including the flowerpot and the row of file cabinets against one wall, William surmised this room to be an office of sorts. He rushed toward the pot of forget-me-nots.

He played with the flowers for quite a while. He enjoyed their distinctive scent and their soft petals. People walked in and out of the room, but none of them saw or bothered him. After a long time of rolling in the petals, he finished with the flowers and flew toward the window.

He knew he went to the same spot he had flown in, but he crashed into the glass. He could not see the glass, so he searched all around, continuing to crash into the window.

It was no use. One of the people must have shut the

window. William grew weary. He began to crawl on the glass, hoping to find an opening. He felt certain there had to be one somewhere.

William's antennae wriggled as he heard a woman's scream fill the office. William looked up to see two women wearing business suits, one of which continued her scream. They both watched him from a safe distance.

'They've seen me!' William thought. The thought frightened him. He decided to try flying again so he could look for the exit faster. The women calmed down, and spoke quietly to each other.

William landed on the window again and listened in to their conversation. He buzzed toward them when they came too close. When he did that, he found they would back away quickly. He wasn't afraid of any humans! He would sting them if they came too near.

"I'm allergic to bee-stings, Saundra," the woman who had so recently screamed now whispered.

"Don't worry Lucinda," Saundra replied. "I called the janitor, and he's going to get it with the shop-vac."

'What's a shop-vac?' William wondered.

The janitor walked into the office. He wore gray overalls and a black baseball cap with a picture of a tarantula spider on it. He pulled what looked like a tall, yellow, plastic garbage can on four small wheels out of the corner of the office. The garbage can had a hose attached to it, making it resemble an aardvark. William liked garbage cans. They sometimes smelled sweet and had tasty stuff inside.

The two women ran next to the janitor. Saundra spoke to him. "Thanks for coming, Earl. The bee is over there by the window."

"I'll get it," Earl promised as he plugged the shop-vac into a wall outlet and then pulled it toward William. The noise from its squeaky wheels hurt William's antennae. He used his antennae like humans use their ears, and sharp noises bothered them.

Earl stood a safe distance from William and hit a switch on the shop-vac. The shop-vac roared loudly. This scared and agitated William even further. He wondered what a shop-vac was, exactly. William decided to try to scare Earl away. He didn't really want to sting the man, but he needed to defend himself against the shop-vac.

Earl waved the end of the hose at William, but the janitor did not seem to be attempting to hit him with it. William avoided it easily, but he felt a little bit of a wind pull at the hair on his back.

William tried to fly away again. Whatever a shop-vac was, it made him nervous. It wasn't a flyswatter. That was for sure! He flew into the window again, hitting it over-and-over in a desperate attempt to escape.

William felt the hair on his neck wriggle. In an instant, the light turned into a small hole surrounded by darkness! The hole and the light disappeared. William hit the sides of what he knew to be the tube. The tube had sucked him inside. A shop-vac must be an animal like an anteater. William realized the shop-vac ate him.

William remembered the time he accidentally flew into a man's mouth. It was all wet, and he didn't like it at all. The man spit William out, and he had to dry off before he could fly again.

Being inside the shop-vac's mouth wasn't like that at all. The shop-vac's mouth was a dry, dusty, long tube instead of a short, wet cavern. It scared William even more than being in the man's mouth.

The shop-vac stopped roaring, but William kept falling down the tube. His earlier attempts to escape from the janitor's attacks wore him out, and he felt too tired and sore to move his wings. Plus, the journey down the tube made him so sore from hitting the sides, he couldn't do much of anything until he rested.

William finally left the tube. He fell into a dark, open space. He thought this must be the shop-vac's stomach. He tried to flap his wings, but they only buzzed weakly. He had landed in a sticky, stringy mess.

As his eyes adjusted to the dim light, William recognized the sticky, stringy mess that caught him. A spider had built a web here! He struggled with all his remaining strength to free himself. He flapped his wings and wiggled his legs, but his attempts only served to entangle him more. He soon realized he shouldn't struggle, but by that time, the web held him fast.

William stopped struggling and remained quite still, but the web began to vibrate. A spider much larger than William crawled down the web toward him. The spider wasn't just one color as spiders often are. A red and white swirl colored the spider, so that he resembled a peppermint candy. The spider frightened William, and he forgot to stay still. He struggled to free himself from the web, but only succeeded in wrapping himself in extra layers of the spider's web.

"Stop struggling!" the spider yelled to him. "You'll only make it harder to get you out again!"

William stopped struggling, and yelled at the spider, "Stay away! If you come any closer, I'll sting you!"

The spider laughed in a deep voice. "That wouldn't help at all! Bees can only sting once. Then what will you do?"

William saw the spider wasn't stopping. As it approached, William did the only thing he could think of. The spider was nearly there! "Help me!" he cried out, in buzzing tones.

CHAPTER 2

"Help me!" William cried as the spider raised four of its eight, swirl-colored arms into the air to bring them down on the poor bee, hopelessly caught in the spider's web. The spider's trap even covered the bee's stinger, rendering it as useless as its arms, legs, and wings.

"What do you think I'm trying to do?" the spider asked as he started to cut away at the web entangling William.

"I think you're trying to eat me!" William sobbed helplessly.

The spider laughed. "You don't know much about spiders, do you?"

"I know spiders eat bees!" William said. "Spiders eat all kinds of insects!"

The spider nodded his head. "Yes, lots of spiders do that," he agreed. "I don't, though. The thought of eating another bug is disgusting!"

"You don't eat bugs?" William asked. He was glad to hear that. "But spiders don't always tell the truth."

"That's true," the spider admitted. "But why would I lie to a bee already wrapped up in my web?"

"Because I can still sting you," William reminded.

The spider continued to work on freeing William's legs from the web. "You could, but I don't think you will."

The spider was right. Though terrified, William trusted the spider for some reason. "Why did you catch me in the web, if you're not going to eat me?"

"Because," the spider replied, "if you'd fallen all the way down you might have hurt yourself." William's legs were completely free by now. The spider worked on releasing the bee's head and wings. "Besides, I use the net to catch food, too."

"Food?" William became nervous again. "So you are going

to eat me!"

The spider laughed. "I told you, I don't eat insects!"

"Then what do you eat?"

"Oh, I eat bears, and elephants, and lions," the spider replied. "Sometimes, I eat camels."

"You are lying!" William protested, forgetting how frightened he felt. "You could never eat that much in a billion-kijillion years! You're too small."

"I am not lying," said the spider. "I like to eat animal crackers and cinnamon bears!"

William had so forgotten to be afraid, that he didn't notice the spider had freed him and he now stood on top of the web. "Really?" he asked. "Where do you get those?" He remembered eating part of a cinnamon bear once, when a little boy dropped it in the park. It tasted so good.

"From the hose," the spider replied. "I catch them in my web after Earl sucks them up from the floor."

For the first time, William noticed he was free. "I'm loose!" For a moment, he thought of flying away, but he trusted the spider.

"Of course you're loose," the spider replied.

"How come I'm not sticking to the web?" William asked.

"Because I put dust all over it so it's not sticky," the spider said. "That is, unless you fall into it. The center's still sticky. I do that so my friends can visit me."

William looked around for the first time since the shop-vacuum sucked him in. A dim light shined through a dusty plastic window near the top of a large, round room. A pile of dirt covered the bottom of the room. William made out the movements of insects in the gloom below. "Where am I?" he asked.

"You're in the shop-vac," the spider informed, "but we who live here call it Entopia!"

Kevin Noel Olson

CHAPTER 3

"Entopia?" William wondered at the word. It seemed...magical! "What does that mean? I'm confused."

"Oh, are you confused?" the spider asked. "I'm sorry; I was just so excited to meet a new insect! Perhaps I should start at the beginning."

"Please," said William politely.

"A long time ago..."

"How long ago?" William interrupted.

"Before I came to Entopia," the spider replied.

"How long ago was that?"

"Three months ago. If you don't be quiet, I'll never finish this story!"

"Can I ask just one more question?"

"You just did," the spider replied.

"Can I ask another?"

"You just did."

The spider wasn't teasing William. He just couldn't see what William wanted to ask. William figured out how to get out of this problem. "Can I ask two more questions?"

"Yes," the spider replied. "You have one more question you can ask. It's silly to ask someone if you can ask them a question."

"Okay," William said. "What is your name?"

"My name is Swirl," the spider answered.

"Why are you called Swirl?"

"That's three more questions," Swirl protested.

William sighed. "Can I ask a few more questions before you start your story?" he asked.

"Certainly," Swirl agreed with a smile.

"Why are you swirly-colored?" William asked.

"Because I fell into a vat of swirled candy coloring," Swirl replied. "Really, if I can tell you the story about Entopia, you can ask any questions it doesn't answer."

"Oh," said William. "I'm sorry, I'll be quiet now."

Swirl cleared his throat, and began to speak; "A long time ago, there were just a few insects in the shop-vac. Earl likes to suck insects up with the shop-vac. The entire shop-vac," Swirl flourished with four of his arms to indicate the enormous room, "is inside of an even larger building called a factory. They make all kinds of snacks here for vending machines. Candy, potato chips, cookies, what have you. Earl caught me with the vacuum after I fell into the vat of candy coloring, but that's another story. You see, they don't like insects in the factory at all, so Earl keeps catching us.

"But I digress. As I was saying..."

"I know!" William said excitedly as he waved his hand. "I know! 'A long time ago, just a few insects...'"

"Please, don't be rude," Swirl requested. "One of the insects was a fly named Albert. Albert figured a secret way out of the shop-vac. Unfortunately he forgot how he did it so he couldn't tell us, and he couldn't get back in. That is, of course, unless he wanted to get caught again and take the dangerous journey through the Tube."

Swirl cleared his throat once more. "Albert stayed around outside of the shop-vac, but he would visit at the window and tell us the wonders of his explorations.

"Saundra likes to read. Albert would sit on her shoulder and read with her. One day, she came into the office with a book named Utopia. A man named Sir Thomas More had written it years ago. Albert read the book voraciously."

"Voraciously?" William interrupted.

The interruption annoyed Swirl. "Yes. He read the book voraciously; meaning he read every word like he was hungry to read them. Albert had a photographic memory, you see. He would fly over and tell the insects the entire story over the next few days."

"I thought you said Albert forgot how to get in and out of the shop-vac," William interjected. "How could he forget if he had a fantastic memory?"

"Please don't interrupt," Swirl admonished. "As I was saying, Albert told the insects the entire story. He told them by talking through the plastic window. The story was about a round city where people lived in peace and harmony, like we do in the shop-vac. Except, of course, we aren't people.

"Albert had also read in a dictionary once about the word 'entomology', which means the study of insects. He figured since 'mology' sounded like a study word; 'ento' must stand for insects. Albert suggested naming the shop-vac Entopia, since the shop-vac is round like Utopia and a land where insects could live together in peace. Since Earl is always vacuuming up snacks, we have more food than we know what to do with. There's no need to fight each other for anything."

"What happened to Albert?" William asked.

"Oh, Albert?" Swirl's brow furrowed as he tried to remember. "On the day Shauna finished reading Utopia, she left it open on the last page and went to get a soda. Albert flew over to finish reading the book, but Shauna came back and shut it over Albert without seeing him. Then, she left the room. No-one has heard from him since."

William, who earlier could hardly keep from asking questions, fell completely silent. Swirl saw this, and broke the young bee's reflection on the story. "Come on, let's go meet the rest of the gang!"

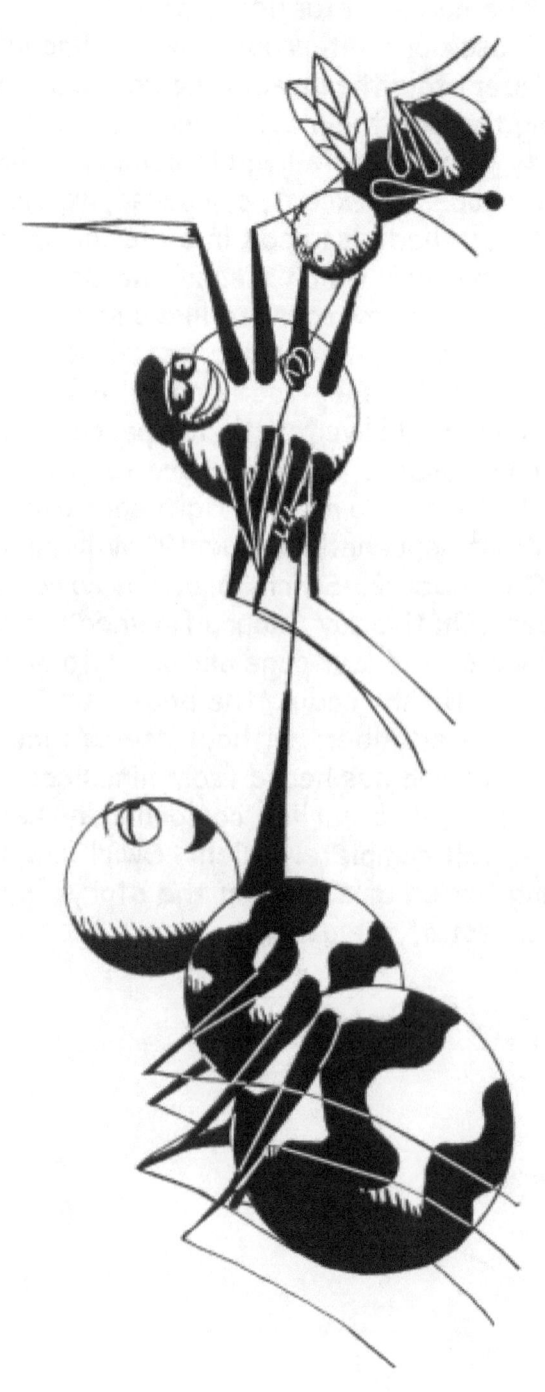

CHAPTER 4

Swirl wrapped his legs around William and started to lower the both of them by a long strand of spider thread. "I'd let you fly down yourself," Swirl said, "but you should get the lay of the land first."

As they descended toward the bottom of the canister, the dim light from the window allowed William's eyes to make out shapes below. He recognized a shiny metal pie-pan atop the center of a massive hill of dirt. Insects moved about, apparently on some sort of business or another.

Swirl released William as soon as the spider's legs touched the top of the pie-pan. "Hello, my friends!" Swirl said, getting the attention of the insects. The bugs stopped their tasks and turned to listen. "I'd like to introduce you to Entopia's newest citizen!"

William felt crowded and nervous as the other insects approached beyond the edge of the pie-pan. William could see the outlines of some of the taller ones, though he could not see their features.

When they had all gathered around, Swirl addressed them. "This, my friends, is William Bee! He has just arrived in Entopia, and I'd like you to extend a warm welcome." A whirring chatter of various, familiar greetings filled the air.

When the sound died down, William felt as if the insects expected him to make a speech. "Glad to be here," he said. "I'm William Bee."

"Can we call you Billy?" a deep voice asked from the crowd.

William could not tell who asked. "Oh, no! I don't think I'd like to be called 'Billy' Bee at all!" he said. "I'd much prefer to be called 'Willy' instead, if it helps."

"Willy it is then!" the voice replied. This time, William

saw it came from a daddy long-leg spider. The spider stepped to the top of the pie-pan and now walked toward him. The spider had seven legs. He had lost his right foreleg and a broken piece of a toothpick replaced it. "My name is Howard," the spider said as he offered his toothpick for a handshake, "but you can call me Toothpick."

William took the offered piece of toothpick and shook it. "Another spider!" he exclaimed in polite surprise. "My, but you're tall!"

Toothpick Howie laughed. "I suppose you could say that."

"Did you lose your leg when you got sucked into the vacuum?" Willy asked.

"Heavens, no!" exclaimed the spider. "I lost it in the wars against the red ants."

Before William could pursue the obvious question, another insect approached. The praying mantis held her arms beneath her sharp chin as she walked along on powerful legs. "Hello, William," she said as she extended her hand. "I am Priscilla."

William accepted the offered hand and shook it. "It's nice to meet you, Priscilla."

"Priscilla's our priest," Swirl interjected. William had nearly forgotten Swirl stood next to him.

"Priest-ess," Priscilla corrected the spider. "I am the spiritual advisor for the entire community," she explained to William.

Meanwhile, yet another insect approached. William instantly recognized it as a large, black beetle. A strong scent of cinnamon came from the insect as he offered his hand. "Hi William! My name is Arnie," the beetle said with his strong, cinnamon breath.

William took the Arnie's hand and shook it. "You're a stinkbug, aren't you?"

Arnie looked ashamed. "Not anymore. After all the cinnamon bears I eat constantly, I only smell like cinnamon."

"I think the cinnamon smells nice," William said. "I don't

mind it at all!"

"I know," Arnie replied. "I'm a stinkbug, you see. You're <u>supposed</u> to mind the smell. It's what we stinkbugs do."

William apologized, "I'm sorry, Arnie. That cinnamon smell is a bit strong."

"Really?" Arnie asked. "Do you think so?"

"Yes, I do," William smiled. "You like to eat the cinnamon bears?"

"Just the bodies," Arnie informed. "Priscilla likes to eat them, too."

"Only the heads," Priscilla pointed out. "Between the two of us, we don't waste anything."

After Priscilla explained, a caterpillar approached the gathering. She had long, pointed hair all down her back tied neatly into ponytails. A pleasant blue color defined her skin beneath. "Hello, I am Cindy," the caterpillar said as she approached.

Swirl broke in again to explain. "Cindy is a caterpillar. She will someday turn into a butterfly!" the spider announced proudly.

"Someday," the caterpillar agreed. Her large eyes drooped sadly. "I haven't yet, though. I've cocooned several times, and each time I only come out as a caterpillar again."

"I'm sure you'll turn into a butterfly soon," William tried to console the caterpillar.

"It won't be too soon," Cindy said with a sniffle.

William surveyed the crowd around him. "Have I met everyone?"

As if in answer, a thin, towering, whip-like black object with a sharp point at the end appeared high in the air beyond the edge of the pie-pan. William recognized it instantly as a scorpion's tail. "Not everyone," Swirl said in a low voice.

The scorpion's tail circled the edge of the pan, apparently looking for a convenient way to climb to the top. The other insects formed a smaller grouping in the center of the pan. "Maybe he can't climb up," Arnie the stinkbug said hopefully.

"Oh, he'll climb up all right," Priscilla replied. Just as she said this, the scorpion's tail stopped. Skittering sounds came from the tail's direction, and soon a pair of red claws appeared over the pie-pan's edge. They opened and closed in rhythm.

Soon, the scorpion's beady eyes appeared, followed by its entire body. The large scorpion moved across the top of the pie-pan. It was at least three times the size of any of the other insects, including Swirl. It had a black body, all except his red claws. Its eight legs clattered across the pie-pan toward the others.

As the scorpion rushed at them, the other insects cringed. William stepped forward. "Hello," he said. "My name is William."

The scorpion came to a halt inches from William's face. William felt its hot breath disturb the hair on his head. "You are not frightened?" the scorpion asked.

"Should I be?" William replied.

"Everyone else is," the scorpion said.

William shrugged. "I just don't know any better, I guess."

The scorpion rested in his spot for a moment. In this time, he looked like a statue that hadn't moved in decades. Then, the scorpion let out a low, rumbling laugh. "It is good to meet you, William," it said. "My name is Gordon, but you can call me Gordon," Gordon said as he extended his large, sleek claw. William looked confused, so Gordon set the record straight, "Or you can call me Gordon, if that works for you."

"I think I'll call you Gordon," William said as he accepted the claw and shook.

"That will do, too," Gordon approved.

The handshake finished, Swirl spoke to William. "Gordon is the only one of us who remembers the world before this. Isn't that right Gordon?"

"That's true," Gordon admitted, "but that's all you

know."

Swirl nodded. "I know, you won't tell us anymore." Swirl smiled widely and clapped his hands together. "Well, I think William's arrival calls for a celebration!" He leaned over to William and said quietly, "That might be the best way for you meet the Katydid twins."

CHAPTER 5

William toured Entopia with Swirl as the other insects prepared the welcome party. Swirl showed him as much of the shop-vac as could be shown, though admittedly, it really wasn't very much at all. Swirl explained how the Katydid twins had chewed the straw sucked into the shop-vac and made bricks and pavement out of it. Swirl and the others had used the bricks to pave the road and build buildings. A few simple, low buildings made up houses and other necessary structures in Entopia.

Swirl pointed out the largest building in Entopia; City Hall. Like the others, it was a low building, but it had a short tower with an old watch pressed into the brick. Though the clock tower didn't work, Swirl showed excessive pride when speaking of it.

Most of the insects lived in burrows underground. A large sinkhole rested in a remote area of the shop-vac where nobody built houses. This provided a garbage dump for Entopia; anything dropped in it would sink and disappear overnight. William, being curious, asked how that happened, but Swirl had no satisfactory answer.

By the time the tour concluded, the other insects had prepared the party. Swirl and William arrived from touring a burrow to see that night had fallen. Six fireflies of various colors flew high above the city. The fireflies each glowed a different color; blue, yellow, red, green, orange, and white. They created a dazzling display.

"Wow," William said to the blue firefly, "that's quite a show!" The firefly just blinked a few times.

"They don't speak," Swirl informed him. "They just blink a code to communicate. He said 'thank you'."

"Wow!" William said. "How did you know?"

"It's a simple code that depends on how long or short

the flashes are," Swirl informed. "I'll teach you sometime."

Snacks had been set around the edge of the pie-pan, and the insects stood around it, eating and talking to each other. On the ground, insects danced about as the Katydids rubbed their back legs together and droned a listless song.

"There aren't many notes to that song," William observed.

"No, there aren't," Swirl agreed. "It's because we don't have enough insects that can sing." Swirl looked thoughtfully at William for a moment. "Can you sing, William?"

William shook his head. "I'm only a bee. I can only sing three notes."

"Which three?" Swirl asked.

William shrugged. "B flat, B sharp, and B natural," he said. "That's not enough to make a song."

Swirl stared at William in silent amazement until it made William uncomfortable. "What?" the young bee asked, but Swirl only turned away and shouted, "Hey everyone! William can sing an A sharp, a B and a C!"

Many insects turned to listen to Swirl. They clapped loudly following his revelation.

"I only said I could sing the B notes," William admonished quietly. "I can't sing an A sharp or a C!"

Swirl turned to him. "A B sharp is a C natural, and a B flat is an A sharp. You said you could sing both!"

"They are?" William asked, confused.

"Yes," Swirl replied. "We don't have anyone in our choir that can sing a B or a C! You'll fit right in."

Toothpick led a group of insects toward William. Toothpick wore a black top hat on his round head, and he looked very dapper in his tailcoat falling off the back of his round body. He wore a white shirt beneath the coat, accented with a black bowtie.

"Very good, Willy!" Toothpick said as he approached. The other insects moved into formation around William. "Now we can sing the Entopia anthem the way it was meant to be sung, in the key of C major!"

"But I don't know the song," William protested.

Toothpick handed him a sheet of paper. "You can read, can't you?"

"Yes," William said, "of course I can read!"

"Good!" Toothpick smiled broadly across his oval face. "That will make it easier. Now, when I point my toothpick above your head," he emphasized this with a demonstration, "I want you to sing a C natural."

"You mean a B sharp?"

"Yes. They are both the same thing. Now, pay attention. When I point toward you but at the ground, I want you to sing an A natural."

"I can only sing a B flat," William pointed out.

"Can you add one more flat to your B flat?" Toothpick inquired.

"I don't know," William said.

"Try it."

William sang a B flat.

"Very good," Toothpick encouraged. "Now, add another flat to your B flat."

William tried to sing a B flat with a flat added, but it felt too low. "I can't do it."

"Sure you can!" Toothpick said. "Sing your B flat and hold it." William did. "Now add another flat." William found himself dropping the note another flat.

"Very good!" Toothpick said. "There you have an A natural!"

William grinned widely. "I did it, didn't I?"

Toothpick nodded. "Now, when I point directly at you, I want you to sing a B natural. Those are all the notes you have to sing. I'll sing the lower notes, and the Katydids will play the higher notes."

William nodded. He was still pleased with his newfound ability to sing a B flat with an extra flat added, or in other words an A natural.

"Good!" Toothpick said. "Now, get in formation with the rest of the choir."

The katydids opened a spot for William. He went to stand with them. Toothpick's eyes became small slits and his lips thinned. He tapped his toothpick forearm against his other forearm, gently bringing it down.

The Katydid twins on the end of the row began singing softly, "Katydid, katydid, katydid," in response to Toothpick's motion. Thus began the Entopia anthem.

William followed along on the sheet, but found no words to sing. The sheet listed words for other parts, but the sheet listed William's part as simply notes. He decided he must sing it as shown on the sheet.

Toothpick sang in a low voice, "If I were," at which point Toothpick pointed to the ground in front of William.

William sang his A natural, or B flat with an added flat. "A," he sang. Then, Toothpick pointed directly at William. "B," William obeyed the signal. Toothpick sang a low word, "You." Directly following, Toothpick pointed over William's head. "C," William sang. He began to understand.

William's notes were also words; a, be or bee, and see or sea. So, the combined voices created the verse; "If I were a bee, you see." This continued throughout the entire song, which went as follows:

(Katydid, katydid, katydid.)

If I were a bee, you see,
I'd want to be in Ent-op-ia!
For to see a bee, happy like me,
You'd have to be, in Ent-op-ia!

(Katydid, katydid, katydid.)

Like clams in the sea, we live a life to be,
Happy as can be, in Ent-op-ia!

We all share, and help to see,
A life good as can be, in Ent-op-ia!

(Katydid, katydid, katydid.)

William looked up when the song finished. "That's a nice song, Toothpick," he said to the conductor as the rest of the choir moved away.

"Yes, and you did a lovely job singing your part!" Toothpick congratulated.

"I wish I could feel that way about Entopia," William admitted.

Swirl and Toothpick both looked at him. "You mean you don't like it here?" Swirl asked.

"Oh no," William denied. "That's not what I mean at all! I just miss the flowers, and my family."

Swirl nodded. "I understand. We've all lost friends and family from the outside, but Entopia can be your new family if you'll allow us."

"I only wish I could choose to live here or not," William said. "It would be one thing if I decided to live here."

"There is no way out of Entopia," Toothpick said. "We've all searched for the way out."

"Albert got out, didn't he?" William asked.

"Yes," Swirl agreed, "but nobody has found out how. Albert didn't tell us."

"Maybe we can look for it again," William said.
"Maybe," Swirl said. "Maybe, but not tonight. It's too dark, and the party is just starting!"

Toothpick waved his wooden arm, beckoning William to follow. "Yes! Let's go enjoy the camaraderie of Entopia!"

William and Swirl followed the gangly daddy long-leg spider into the party. William enjoyed the party immensely as he met new insects and enjoyed the banquet. Katydids played their repetitive, but beautiful, music throughout the night.

CHAPTER 6

The party lasted late into the night, so William awoke later in the morning. Swirl had not yet found accommodations for William. Meanwhile, he had slept on top of the pie-pan. Dusty rays of sunlight seeped in through the single, dirty window of the shop-vac and fell across his face. He rubbed his eyes and looked about.

Already, the insects moved about on their business. Swirl carried food deliveries from house to house while Priscilla taught a pair of young fireflies near the town hall. Toothpick walked down the street, stabbing his pointed wooden arm into discarded trash and placing it in a recycled candy bag.

"Good morning!" Swirl shouted as he walked toward William. "How did you sleep?"

"I slept well," William replied. "Thank you."

Just then, the shop-vac roared to life and unexpectedly disrupted the calm morning.

Swirl looked up suddenly. "Oh no!" he exclaimed. "Everyone! Get under the pie-pan!"

Most insects had already started for the pie-pan, which Toothpick lifted and propped up with his wooden arm. "Hurry up!" he shouted to the approaching insects, as he detached the wooden arm and left it. "It's going to start hailing soon!"

Arnie, the cinnamon stinkbug walked on top of the pie-pan, making a ringing sound to create an alarm for all the insects who might not have heard the warnings.

The fireflies headed for their burrows underground. They preferred the darkness so they could light it.

The flurry of activity bewildered William, and left him unsure of what to do.

"Come on!" Swirl said as he scooped William up in his large jaws and carried him. "We've got to get to the shelter!"

The clattering sound of something sucked through the hose joined the noise of the shop-vac's roar. The alarm stopped ringing as Arnie retreated under the pie-pan.

Carrying William in his jaws slowed Swirl considerably. Candy, sticks, and small pebbles began to fall from the hose. Swirl neared the pie-pan with his burden when a large, yellow object broke through the web above and struck Swirl harshly on the back of his head. Swirl fell unconscious to the ground, dropping William from his jaws in the process.

"Get in here, Willy!" shouted Toothpick over the roar of the shop-vac.

"But what about Swirl?" William protested. "He's hurt!"

Toothpick shook his head. "There's nothing you can do for him! He's too heavy! Get in here!"

"No!" the young bee replied. The deadly hail continued through the hole in the spider-web. William grasped Swirl's front leg and tried to drag the spider to safety. He pulled and pulled, but he couldn't budge Swirl. He closed his eyes and tugged extra hard. Amazingly, he could feel Swirl moving! He was doing it! He was pulling Swirl to safety!

Then, William heard a female voice say, "We're inside now, William. You can stop pulling now."

William opened his eyes to see Priscilla still clutched three of Swirl's legs in her powerful arms. He hadn't saved Swirl alone.

The shop-vac stopped its roar, and the last few items clattered off the top of the pie-pan. "Thanks," William said to Priscilla.

"No, thank you," the praying mantis replied as she carefully examined the wound on Swirl's head. "He might have been killed out there, but thanks to you, he might be alright."

Toothpick lifted the pie-pan. "All clear!" he said after looking out. The insects started filing out of the pie-pan. The fireflies emerged from their burrows beneath the ground, and Priscilla called them over. "We've got wounded over here!" she said. "Swirl needs to go to the hospital!"

The fireflies headed toward the pie-pan to act as an ambulance for the fallen mayor of Entopia. All six of them picked him up and carried him to the hospital. They couldn't fly with the heavy spider.

"Will he be okay?" William asked Priscilla.

She nodded. "He's going to be fine. The roach doctor will fix him."

"Entopia has a roach doctor?" William asked as the ants loaded Swirl onto a stretcher.

"Yes," Priscilla said. "Who better a doctor than someone who can survive for weeks without his head?"

"The roach doctor doesn't have a head?" William asked. "How can he operate without eyes?"

Priscilla laughed. "Of course he has a head! He has a name, too..."

"Paul," a gruff voice interrupted Priscilla. A roach walked around the edge of the pie-pan and stopped the fireflies. He wore a long white coat and a round mirror on his head (which was, in fact, only a piece of a round, silver candy like those on birthday cakes). "Doctor Paul Roche," he said without looking at anyone but the patient.

Dr. Roche examined the knot on Swirl's head. "Quite a bump, but I don't think it's necessary to bring him to the hospital. He'll be fine."

As if on cue, Swirl moaned. He sat up and searched his surroundings. "What happened?" he groaned as he stood. The fireflies left with Doctor Paul.

Priscilla smiled at him. "You were hit on the head by a lemon drop," she said.

"While you were trying to rescue me!" William interjected.

Swirl nodded. "I remember that part."

"William rescued you," Priscilla said.

William's eyes grew wide. "I didn't," he denied. "Priscilla carried you in."

"Still," Priscilla replied, "he did try to save you, and

you were saved. I think he deserves the credit."

"Well," Swirl began, "thank you both." He pointed at the lemon drop still on the ground. "Is this the lemon drop that hit me?"

William nodded. "That's the one."

Suddenly, a muffled voice came from the lemon drop. "I am not a lemon drop!" it said in protest.

All three looked at the lemon drop. "The lemon drop talks!" William exclaimed.

"Of course I talk!" the lemon drop said. "And I am not a lemon drop!"

Swirl moved toward it. "This could be a trick," he said. "Let's see if it tastes like a lemon drop."

"No! No!" the lemon drop said. It shuddered. "Please, don't eat me!"

Swirl stood over the lemon drop, examining it. Priscilla and William joined him.

"I'm not a lemon drop," the lemon drop repeated wearily. "I'm a sugar ant, and a vacuunaut."

"A vacuunaut?" Priscilla asked. "What's that?"

"We travel the unknown space of vacuums," the lemon drop informed. "Vacuum cleaners remain a vast mystery to us sugar ants. When we return from this deadly journey, we tell others what we've found."

"What have you found before?" William asked.

The lemon drop rolled a bit. "I don't know. No one has ever returned from a vacuum."

"Why should we believe you?" Swirl demanded.

"Just break open the lemon drop," the voice replied. "You'll see I'm telling the truth."

Swirl opened his jaws wide and picked up the lemon drop.

"Don't eat it!" William exclaimed.

"Yes," the lemon drop agreed. "Don't eat me!"

Swirl just shook his head as he lifted the lemon drop with his teeth. The powerful jaws clamped down, and the lemon drop broke in half. A tiny, bright orange ant fell to the ground.

"Thank you!" the ant said. "My name is Adam." He put forth his hand.

William accepted the gesture and shook hands. "Glad to meet you, Adam. My name is William."

"William!?" the ant replied. "Are you certain?"

"Of course I'm certain," William replied.

"And you're a bee?" Adam asked.

"Of course I'm a bee!" William replied. "What else would I be?"

"I'm just making sure," Adam said. "You see, we are holding a young bee prisoner. We caught him in our hill searching for his older brother, William."

William's heart sank. "What was his name?"

"He said his name was Robert," Adam replied. "He told us about how sweet the bee's honey is, and now our queen wants to attack the beehive for its honey. She thinks it will go nicely with the aphid milk we captured from another colony of ants."

"That's horrible!" Swirl said.

Adam nodded. "I agree; but an ant does what he is ordered to do. What else can he do?"

"He can fight," William said.

"Fight my own hill?" Adam said. "I won't fight against my brother ants."

"There are other ways to fight," Swirl informed.

William turned to Swirl. "I've got to get out of here," he said. "I've got to save my brother from the sugar ants and warn the beehive!"

"But there's no way out of the shop-vac!" Swirl informed.

"Albert got out," William said. "There must be a way."

Swirl nodded. "There is a way," he agreed, "but no-one knows what it is."

"We must search," William said. "If there is a way out,

we can find it."

Swirl shrugged. "How are we going to find it?" he asked. "I don't even know where to begin."

William's eyes lighted. "Mom always told me if I couldn't find something look where I lost it!"

"What does that mean?" Adam asked.

"Well," William said, "if I lost something, I should remember as far back as I could and remember the last time I had it. Then, I could retrace my steps."

"We can't do that," Swirl said. "We weren't here at the beginning. We don't remember where it was lost."

"Gordon the scorpion says he remembers the world before this world!" William reminded. "To start at the beginning, we need to ask some who was there!"

Swirl nodded. "That's it!" he said. "Let's go ask Gordon!"

The three walked toward the scorpion's burrow. Adam and Swirl seemed apprehensive as they followed William to Gordon's den.

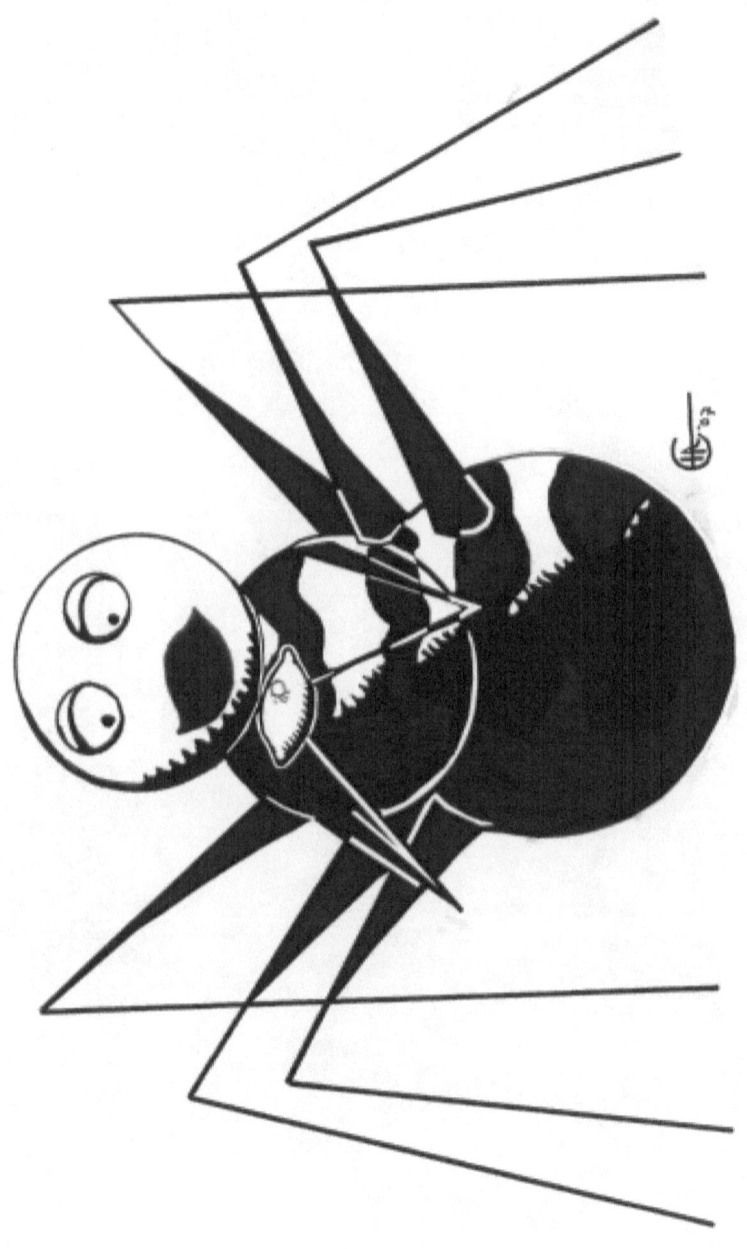

CHAPTER 7

William stepped to the trapdoor covering Gordon's den and knocked. Adam and Swirl stood a reasonable distance away.

No reply came for a few minutes to William's initial knock, so he knocked again.

"Maybe he's not home," Adam said. "That would be nice."

As if in answer to Adam's statement, the door swung wide. William moved to avoid being struck. A pair of red claws stretched forth from the hole. William could see a pair of eyes peering through the darkness like glowing red beads. "Hello," Gordon's voice boomed.

"Hello," William replied. "We need information about the world before this world."

Gordon moved from inside the hole with incredible speed. Swirl and Adam stepped back slightly, but the scorpion halted in front of William. "Are you sure you want to know?" he asked as he looked sidelong in the spider's direction.

"Yes," William replied. "We need to know."

Gordon turned back toward the door of his den. "Follow me," he said as he slipped back into the hole. "I will tell all I know."

William followed Gordon into the hole. Swirl and Adam looked at each other, then at the hole. With some reluctance, they followed William.

It took a moment to adjust to the dimness of the hole, but a few fireflies shared the den with Gordon and illuminated the interior adequately. The increased darkness failed to bother either William or his companions. Insects rely on other senses than simply sight, and William used his antennae to feel along the walls as easily as he would in the beehive.

Gordon folded his legs on the far end of the large, round room of which his den consisted. Swirl, Adam and

William sat on the other side of the room.

"So," Gordon began, "what do you want to know about the world before this world?"

"We need to know how Albert escaped the shop-vac," William said.

"You think I know that," Gordon surmised, "because I was here in the world before this world."

"I hope you know," William said.

Gordon shook his head. "I know how Albert got out," he said. "It has little to do with the world before. I will tell you about the world before, and worlds before that. More worlds than I can count, all much like Entopia."

William now regretted having asked about the world before. He only wanted to know how Albert the fly escaped, but he did not interrupt the scorpion as he spoke.

"You see," Gordon began after a deep sigh, "every once in a while Earl the janitor empties the canister vacuum."

"Empties?" Swirl said, horrified at the thought. "What do you mean?"

"I mean, Swirl," Gordon explained, "he takes the lid off the shop-vac and empties the contents into the dumpster outside the snack factory."

"But what happens to Entopia when he empties the shop-vac?" Swirl asked.

"Entopia goes into the dumpster," Gordon explained. "I do not know what happens after that."

"But," Adam interjected, "that's horrible!"

Gordon shook his head. "No, it is not horrible. You see, Entopia is simply one civilization that will be replaced by another civilization."

"Well," Swirl said with wet eyes, "I suppose the next will be even better than Entopia."

"Perhaps," Gordon said. "Perhaps not. A civilization is the creation of its citizens. I've seen quite a few worse in my time, and a couple nearly as good as this one, but none better than Entopia."

"You said you've seen some nearly as good, but none better?" William said.

"Yes," Gordon replied. "There are many good ways to run a civilization. There are even more bad ways to run one. Then, there are all sorts of civilizations in between."

"Am I to understand," Swirl put in, "you are unhappy with the way Entopia runs?"

"It could be better," Gordon admitted. "Still, I am quite pleased with Entopia's government. This might seem hard to understand, but I do not believe we are truly living up to our insect nature."

"How do you mean?" Adam asked.

"Take me, for instance," Gordon said. "I am a hunter by birth. In Entopia, I cannot hunt."

"All citizens should be protected," Swirl said.

Gordon nodded. "I agree. It is not the government that keeps me from hunting, it is the nature of the shop-vac itself. When I grew up in the uranium mine, there were large bugs to hunt and fight. Surviving wasn't easy outside the shop-vac. Hunting as a captured insect in such a small space would defeat the purpose of hunting altogether. There would be no challenge."

Swirl nodded. "I see what you mean."

"I am uncertain whether or not Entopia is good for any of us," Gordon mentioned. "Perhaps the insects that would normally be hunted outside are missing out on something too."

"How did you get from the world before to this world?" William asked.

Gordon deepened his voice. "I can always tell when the shop-vac is about to be emptied because Earl rolls it across the rough pavement outside. I held onto a piece of wire on the side of the shop-vac with my tail." He pointed to a piece of wire holding a paper price tag in the corner of the room attached securely to the side of the canister. No one had noticed before that one side of the room was actually the side of the shop-vac. "I have seen more worlds come and go than Entopia has citizens."

"If there is a way out," William said, "we might save the citizens of Entopia by evacuating them before it happens."

Gordon shook his head. "There is a way, but you would not be listened to if you told them the truth. I have only seen Albert escape."

"We will make them go!" Swirl said passionately.

"That is not what Entopia is about," Gordon replied as he looked into Swirl's face. "Entopia exists because bugs choose for themselves. Would you save Entopia by destroying its foundations?"

Swirl's features dropped. "No, of course not," he replied.

"But Swirl," William said, "I can't leave one community in peril to go and save another."

"What did you say?" Gordon asked.

"I've got to get out of Entopia to save my little brother," William said, "and my beehive is in danger from the sugar ants."

Swirl suddenly stood to his feet. "Perhaps, my young friend," Swirl said to William, "we can do both at once!"

"Yes!" Gordon exclaimed. "I see your plan! It just might work!"

"I don't understand," William said.

"Me neither," Adam admitted.

"I'm sorry," Swirl turned to the pair, "but I've got to tell everyone at once. We've got to call a town meeting!"

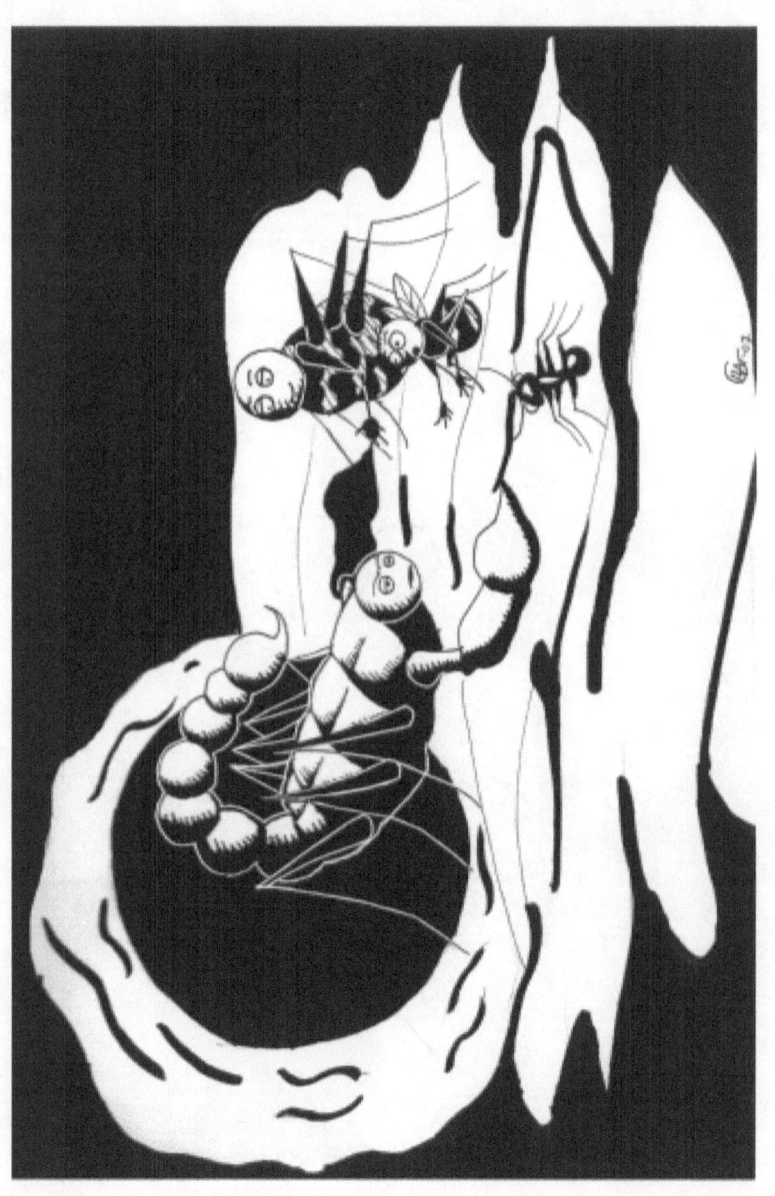

CHAPTER 8

Within the next hour, Arnie stomped back and forth across the pie-pan to sound an alert for the town meeting. The clattering noise attracted the citizens of Entopia, who gathered around the pie-pan. When he was finished, he'd made the entire area smell of cinnamon by breathing heavily.

Swirl mounted the pie-pan, and Arnie took it as a cue to leave. "Thank you Arnie," Swirl said as the cinnamon bug left. He turned to the audience where it congregated the thickest. "Greetings, citizens of Entopia!" he said, rather dramatically.

The insects cheered for a long moment, then fell silent. The mayor continued his speech. "I have brought you together to discuss the future of Entopia. We have built a grand civilization from our misfortune. We have taken what little we were given, and we have made so much more than was possible. The achievements attained during Entopia's short history have been monumental in stature."

This statement produced another uproar of approval. "Unfortunately," Swirl continued, "it has been brought to my attention that things outside Entopia go poorly for others. The beehive and the anthill stand on the brink of war, with nothing standing in its way."

"What does that have to do with us?" one of the katydid twins asked.

Swirl shook his head. "Nothing," he replied. "It positively, absolutely, has nothing at all to do with Entopia and its citizens. Only that we have, as a community, promised to make our immediate world a place where insects can live in peace. Life, I will remind you all, is difficult enough without adding unnecessary wars to complicate matters. The sugar ants have decided to invade the beehive to obtain the honey that is not rightfully theirs, and that the bees would likely trade to the sugar ants if approached on friendly and fair terms. It is my proposal that the Entopians help the bees in this war."

"Why not the ants?" asked Adam. "Why are we siding with the bees?"

Swirl nodded in acknowledgment of the ant's concern. "Certainly, we would aide the anthill in defending itself against violent aggression. However, the sugar ants are attacking without provocation other than the greed of their queen."

"You've stated," Toothpick said, "there's no reason to make life more difficult by starting a war, yet you propose to join one. How is that helping the Entopians?"

"This is not a move to help the Entopians," Swirl replied. "This would be to show the world what it means to live in peace and progress as Entopians live."

"Be that as it may," the daddy long-leg spider continued, "you've left out one point. To help the beehive, we would have to leave Entopia, perhaps forever."

Swirl swallowed hard and nodded. He forced back tears as he spoke, "No, we would not have to leave Entopia." He spread his arms out to indicate the surrounding area. "What you see here is not Entopia. It is the shop-vac." He brought his hands down to his chest. "Entopia lives here, in our hearts and minds.

"You see, Entopia is not a place. Entopia is an idea. Our purpose to bring peace and prosperity to other insects reflects that idea. Our actions reflect that purpose. We can rebuild the location of Entopia in the world outside. Certainly, there may not be the abundance of food and protection from the weather as we have experienced here, but we can create a land where insects live in peace in the harshest environment."

"But what will happen to our city?" asked Dr. Roche. "We've built hospitals, places of worship, government buildings, and even buildings dedicated to insectarian causes.

What will happen to those?"

Swirl glanced toward Gordon for strength, but Gordon's head fell. Swirl cleared his throat and said, "All this will be destroyed soon."

The crowd gasped. "Destroyed?" Priscilla said. "What are you talking about?"

"Every once in a while," Swirl answered, "Earl the janitor empties the shop-vac. When that happens, everything we've been able to build and everyone residing in it will tumble into the dumpster. We don't know what happens after that."

"What if Earl doesn't empty the shop-vac?" Priscilla continued her line of questioning.

At this, Gordon shook his head and stepped forward to answer. "Earl always empties the shop-vac eventually," he said. "I don't know when it will happen again, but all I can say is he's emptied it before. I've lost friends, enemies, and even family during these purges."

"I don't believe you!" Cindy the caterpillar shouted. "I don't remember anything like that happening before."

Gordon frowned. "You weren't here when it happened," he replied softly. "Only I've survived the worlds before this world. Other insects didn't believe me either, and the civilizations they created buried them in the dumpster. I survived by holding onto a wire."

"If that's true," said Arnie the stinkbug, "how do we escape?"

"There is a way out," Gordon said, "but it's a dangerous journey, and not for the timid."

"You said you knew how Albert escaped," William reminded.

Gordon nodded. "Yes," the scorpion said, "I saw how Albert got out of Entopia. Albert flies while he's sleeping."

"You mean he's a sleep-flier?" asked William. "I've heard about that, but I didn't think it was real."

Gordon nodded. "Yes, it's very real," he assured. "As I was saying, Albert flew in his sleep. He was flying in his sleep the last time Earl emptied the shop-vac. I watched as everything fell into the dumpster."

"Why didn't Albert get hit by something?" William asked.

Gordon shrugged. "I don't know," he admitted. "Dust and hard-candies flew all around him, but Albert didn't notice any of it. Nothing seemed to touch him. It really was beautiful."

"It sounds like a miracle," William said.

"There are miracles everywhere," Priscilla said as she walked into the conversation. "Miracles are so much a part of our everyday life that we cease to observe the larger part of them. We only take note of the rare occurrences, rather than acknowledging that the true miracle is the fact we are here to experience at all. Everything else only serves to compound that singular and miraculous event of mere existence."

William nodded. "I don't think I understand," he said, but did not pursue the statement. "Gordon, how does Albert's escape help us?"

"It doesn't," Gordon replied.

"But you said you knew how to escape," William protested.

"Yes, I did," Gordon said. "Albert's escape is not the only way I know."

"How do we get out, then?" William asked.

"Albert's escape gave me an idea," the scorpion replied. "We fly out."

"Fly out? But the fireflies, Priscilla and I are the only insects in all Entopia that can fly!" William reminded.

Gordon shook his head. "No, you're the only insects that have wings. Earl sucked a broken balloon into the shop-vac after Saundra's last birthday. I kept it in my house. Swirl, can you patch up a balloon with spider webs?"

"I sure could!" Swirl responded.

"Good. The next time Earl empties the shop-vac, we'll

fly out."

"You said you didn't know when Earl would empty the shop-vac next," William said. "How long will we have to wait?"

"Well, we won't have to wait long if we make Earl empty it," Gordon said. "Swirl can put a web around the hole, so nothing will be able to get in."

Great plan, Gordon!" Swirl said. "If nothing is coming in, Earl will think it's full!"

"Okay," William nodded. "How are we going to fill the balloon?"

"We'll fill it with Arnie's cinnamon air," Gordon said.

For the first time, William understood the plan. He understood it might work, too. Arnie the stinkbug's defense mechanism allowed him to release bad-smelling breath. Since it smelled like cinnamon now, it wasn't toxic. The insects wouldn't have to be in the balloon long anyhow. Their small numbers should allow it to fall slower than the rest of the garbage. Anything that might hit them would bounce off the balloon and they would fall softly into the dumpster. He thought it might work, and he only had one more question, "When can we start?"

"If we're going to save your brother," Gordon replied, "we should start right away!"

CHAPTER 9

46

They did start right away. Gordon pulled the broken balloon out of his house. It looked like a long, flat, blue earthworm. Swirl immediately started patching the hole in it. When he was done, Arnie came along to begin filling it with cinnamon air.

While Arnie filled the balloon, Cindy began weaving caterpillar silk around the outside to re-enforce the balloon. Swirl went off to cover the opening to the shop-vac so nothing could get in while the insects carried cinnamon bears to Arnie to keep him fed. When Arnie had filled the balloon, Toothpick sealed a makeshift cardboard door to the opening with a spider web.

It took all day, but the insects accomplished a lot in that time. Gordon nodded his approval as he examined the balloon. "Very nice," he said. "Now, all we have to do is wait for Earl to empty the shop-vac." The large, blue sphere seemed quite regal in the dim sunlight. Cindy had used her silk to place the word Entopia on the outside of the balloon in large letters.

The insects did not have to wait long. Earl pulled the shop-vac out in the morning, while the insects began piling into the balloon. The larger insects had to stretch the opening a little bit to enter, but the smaller insects made it through with ease. Swirl and Gordon were the last insects inside. Toothpick wrapped his legs around the balloon opening to seal it off. Some cinnamon-scented air escaped the balloon while the insects entered, but Arnie easily refill it.

The shop-vac's motor roared to life for a few moments. The insects watched through the transparent blue balloon as the webbing Swirl had put in place stretched under the pressure of whatever Earl vacuumed. The motor turned off after a while. The shop-vac started to move again. In a moment, it began to rumble loudly as Earl pulled the shop-vac over the rough pavement outside. The lid lifted off the shop-vac. Sunlight streamed through the balloon-walls.

"Here we go," Gordon announced as Earl lifted the shop-vac. Dirt, candy, and everything Earl had sucked into the shop-vac bounced off the top of the balloon as the janitor emptied the contents. The balloon fell slower than the other contents of the shop-vac, eventually coming to rest on top of a pile of papers.

William looked around to ensure nobody had been hurt. "We made it!" he exclaimed. Before anyone could answer, a gust of wind came through the dumpster, lifting the balloon into the air. The balloon continued to float on the wind.

"We are flying!" Priscilla exclaimed. The blue balloon floated over the green lawn. "We are really flying!"

Swirl nodded. "Yes," he mused, "but where are we flying to?"

Priscilla pressed her face against the translucent blue balloon and look outside. "I think we're heading for the river!" she informed. "If we land in it, we could get swept away!"

"If we don't get out of the balloon," Toothpick reminded, "we'll eventually suffocate!"

"Perhaps not," Gordon encouraged. "We could let the gas out of the balloon and drown instead."

Swirl tried to formulate a plan. "Arnie, is there any way you could exhale more cinnamon breath?" he asked.

Arnie shook his head. "No, I'm sorry," he replied in way of apologizing. "The river's too wide and the far bank is too steep. We'll never clear it that way."

"Toothpick," Swirl turned to the daddy long-leg spider and continued, "can you release the air or puncture the balloon? Maybe the air pressure will send us away from the river."

"No," Toothpick replied, "we'd likely fall into the river anyway, and without the gas we'd sink. We couldn't control the balloon at all."

Swirl spun about the center of the balloon looking for

someone who could help. He stopped spinning when he saw Priscilla looking at him. "I guess that's it," he said, hanging his head.

"We can hold a thought," Priscilla said as the balloon drew near the surface of the river.

Gently, the balloon landed on the water. The lazy current pulled it downstream. William looked out the side of the balloon. "Where does it go?" he asked.

Swirl shrugged a reply. "I don't know," he admitted. "I think it just keeps on going forever."

"That's not true," Gordon countered. "Most waterways eventually end up in a large body of water. Unfortunately, they sometimes turn into waterfalls before they do that."

"We've got to do something," William said.

"Something sometimes does itself," Priscilla reminded.

Suddenly, William heard a low buzzing noise. The noise grew louder by the second. "Look!" William exclaimed as he pointed upstream.

All the insects looked out the balloon. A small, black cloud drifted quickly over the river toward the balloon. It got closer and closer until William said, "It's a cloud of insects!"

Indeed, the cloud flew over the river. Some of the airborne insects flew within inches of the balloon. The insects looked strange, with long wings and thin, wiry appendages at their tails.

"Mayflies," Priscilla whispered to Swirl.

"Help!" William shouted as they flew by. "Please, help us! It won't take very long!"

None of the insects seemed to hear William, though some looked with vague curiosity at the floating balloon. The swarm passed overhead, and none of the insects stopped. William looked after them. "Help us!" he shouted once more.

"Stop shouting," Toothpick demanded. "It's no use."

William sighed and sat down next to Cindy. "I'm sorry I got us all into this mess," he said.

"What mess?" Cindy asked. "I've never felt so alive! I was born in Entopia, so I've seen more in the past few minutes than I've ever seen!" She smiled brightly. "It's not a mess, it's a life!"

William nodded glumly. Sure, it was enough for a caterpillar who had never known the joys of flying, sunshine, pollinating flowers, or making honey. For him, it was a disaster. If he died now, it would be too young. His head buzzed lightly. He put his hand to his head to try to make it stop, but it didn't. His realized his head wasn't buzzing. He sat up and looked upstream again. A lone mayfly flew toward the balloon!

"Help!" William shouted. "Help us!"

"I told you to quit," Toothpick admonished.

William ignored the comment. "Help us!"

This mayfly noticed and headed toward the balloon. When she got closer, William got his first look at a mayfly. Many words William didn't understand could describe this girl mayfly, but William only thought of one; beautiful!

"Yes?" the girl asked William. "What's wrong?"

"Could you push the balloon to shore?" William asked through the balloon. "I'd do it if I was outside, but from inside it's impossible."

"Sure," the mayfly said, "I'll push you to shore."

With that, she flew next to the balloon and started pushing on it as she flapped her wings wildly.

"Thanks," William said, "I'm William. What's your name?"

The task of pushing the balloon preoccupied the mayfly, but she responded, "April."

William took note of the difficulty of April's task, and decided not to talk to her until they were safely ashore. April pushed the balloon with the current but toward the shore. Soon, she rolled the balloon onto the rocks.

"We made it!" William said.

"Not all of us," Katy Katydid replied. "We found him this way." All eyes looked at her holding Adam, the sugar ant, unconscious in her arms. Her twin sister, Sally Katydid, stood next to her looking at Adam.

"Who found him?" Swirl asked.

Sally looked at Swirl. "Katy did."

Dr. Paul, the roach, pressed through the insects. "Please," he said, "let me through. Maybe I can help." He pulled out a stethoscope made from a piece of licorice-rope and put it on the ant's chest. "He's still breathing!" he said. Everyone breathed a sigh of relief. "He needs some fresh air. I think Arnie's cinnamon air knocked him out. He must have some sort of allergy."

Everyone looked at Toothpick. "Well," he said, "we have to do it some time! We should do it slowly, though."

Keeping his other seven legs wrapped around the nozzle, he lifted his toothpick and put a small hole into the side of the balloon. He quickly jabbed the toothpick through the bottom of the balloon, anchoring it to the soft mud so it couldn't blow away. A thin, whistling sound filled the balloon as cinnamon air exited it in a stream outside.

After the roof had deflated quite a bit, Toothpick let go of the opening. "Everybody out!" he shouted.

As the ceiling sank, Swirl, Priscilla, and Gordon propped it up as the smaller insects left. First, Katy Katydid walked out onto the river-rock carrying Adam. Dr. Paul followed immediately to assist his patient. Other insects soon left until the three largest squeezed through the opening. They all stood on shore next to the deflated balloon.

William walked over to the helpful mayfly. "Thank you, April," he said. "If you hadn't helped us, who knows what would have happened?"

"I'm glad to help," she replied. "Only, I've lost my swarm." She bowed her head and frowned. "I'll never catch up with them now."

"You didn't stay with your swarm so you could help us?" William asked.

April nodded dejectedly. "Yes," she replied.

William felt bad. He now knew why none of the other mayflies stopped. Then, he got an idea. "Say," he said, "we could be your swarm until you find the others."

April's face brightened a little. "You mean, you wouldn't mind?" she asked.

William shook his head. "Of course not," he assured her. "We've all lost family and friends before. That's what this group is about! Insects banding together to help each other. That's what you did for us!"

Swirl walked over. "Yes," he agreed. "April, you have done much to show you have Entopia in your heart!"

"Entopia?" she asked.

"Yes," William said. "I'll explain later. Right now, we are on the wrong side of the river."

Swirl looked about and nodded. "I was just noticing that unfortunate detail myself."

"Well," April interjected, "there is a bridge a little ways up the river."

Gordon walked over and stood next to Swirl. "I don't see anything," the scorpion said. "If it's not close enough to see, it will take us too long to reach it."

"It won't take that long," April said. "Not if we fly!"

Swirl shook his head. "No, the balloon has had it," he pointed out, "and those of us that don't fly have had enough of flying for one lifetime that we weren't meant to fly in."

April nodded. "Sorry, I forgot," she said in way of apology.

"Think nothing of it," Swirl replied. "We just have to find a way across the river without having to go all the way to the bridge."

"What about making our own bridge?" William offered.

Swirl looked at the river. It seemed very wide and very dangerous. "I don't see how we could make a bridge," he said.

"We made an escape from the shop-vac," William pointed out, "surely we can construct a bridge."

"With what?" Gordon interjected. "We don't have any resources!"

"That's not completely true," Swirl said. "I can still make webbing, and Cindy can still make silk," he shook his head again, "but I don't know if we can make enough time to construct an entire bridge." He shook his head. "It would take far too long."

"You're right," William said. "We're going to have to find another way. April, would you come and help me look?"

"Of course," the mayfly replied. Soon, she and William were flying along the bank of the river. "You know," April said, "we could fly over the river ourselves."

William shook his head. "No, I couldn't rescue my little brother and stave off an ant invasion on my beehive without their help. Also, they gave up everything so they could help me. I couldn't let them down now. I've got to get them over the river."

"In that case," April said, "perhaps we need to find a way to get them under the river instead."

"What do you mean?" William asked.

"A lot of these insects are burrowers," April pointed out. "They spend most of their lives burrowing under the earth. Maybe someone has already burrowed under the river."

"I see what you're saying!" William said. "But how would we find a burrow that goes under the river?"

"I just thought of it when I saw that rabbit," April said, pointing at a small, grey rabbit in the tall, green grass. "I saw it on the other side of the river when we were talking to Swirl, and now it's on this side. I don't think it swam over, or it'd be wet. So..."

"So, it went through a burrow!" William said excitedly. "All we have to do is watch where it goes into a burrow! It must go to the other side!"

April and William buzzed about for a while, keeping their eyes locked on the rabbit. In a few moments, their patience paid off. The rabbit disappeared into a hole in the grass. "Eureka!" April exclaimed. "That's where the hole is!" Still, they watched the other side of the river to make certain.

Sure enough, the rabbit scurried out of the grass on the other side of the river. "There it is!" William said. "It will work!" The mayfly and the bee flew to tell the others.

Swirl stood next to Cindy, discussing how they might weave a bridge quickly and safely as William and April landed next to them. "Forget that, Swirl," William said. "We found another way!"

April couldn't contain her excitement as she interrupted William, "Yes! There's a burrow underneath the river!"

"A burrow?" Swirl said. "Where?"

"Just down the shore that way," William pointed behind him. "It's a quick walk, and then under the river!"

"How did you find it?" Swirl pressed.

William shrugged. "We saw the rabbit go in and come out on the other side."

"A rabbit!" Cindy shrieked. "A rabbit might eat us!"

Swirl nodded. "That's right, William. Have you thought of that?" he asked.

William shook his head. "No," he admitted, "I hadn't."

Swirl scratched his chin thoughtfully and looked at William. "Still, I suppose it's the only way," he decided. "Show me the entrance, and I'll inform the others."

In a few moments, William and April showed Swirl the hole the rabbit had disappeared into. "Okay, we'll meet you two on the other side," Swirl said.

"Oh, no you will not. I am going with you," William demanded.

"Me too," April chimed in.

"It will be dangerous," William reminded her. "I want you to fly over to the other side."

"No," April said emphatically. "I will go with everyone else. We'll meet our fates together."

William looked into her eyes and saw how serious she felt. "Okay," he conceded.

In a few moments, all the insects had assembled at the entrance to the burrow. Gordon decided to take the lead. He claimed his experience growing up in a uranium-mine qualified him. Swirl traveled at the back. Cindy made a rope about Priscilla's neck because a praying mantis walks faster than a caterpillar. After taking a deep breath, Swirl disappeared into the hole. William followed close behind and the other insects followed suit.

"It sure is dark in here," Katy Kaydid noted once they began traveling the long corridor. Although it was dark as noted, the insects did not need to utilize their eyesight to maneuver. In any case, the fireflies produced a small but sufficient amount of light.

The burrow proved to be far wider than the hole that led into it. Water dripped from the dirt ceiling, but the size of the burrow made it easy enough to avoid getting wet. Small mud puddles formed on the dirt floor, but these were easy to get around.

Gordon took note of several small holes dug in the side of the burrow. "We're not alone here," he informed the others.

Through the small holes came several garden-snakes. Most did not exceed Gordon's length by much, but there must have been twelve or so in all. They cautiously approached the crew of insects from all sides. One approached Swirl from the front of the tunnel.

"I do not understand," William whispered to Priscilla. "If they live down here, why don't they attack the rabbit?"

"They are too small, I suspect," the praying mantis replied. "They will not attack anything as large as a rabbit. Insects, however, are a different matter."

"What do we do?" April asked.

"I'll do what I always do," Priscilla answered. "Pray."

One of the snakes pulled close to the group and lunged at a firefly. The fly moved deftly out of the way as the snake prepared for another lunge.

"I could use my sting," William offered.

"No," Priscilla said. "You'll die. There must be another way."

"There is," Swirl said and turned to yell, "Gordon! Arnie!"

"With you Swirl!" the scorpion yelled in reply.

"Me too!" yelled the cinnamon stinkbug.

The snakes closed in as Swirl gave one last order, "You know what to do, Priscilla and Toothpick. Get them out of here!"

With this last shout, Swirl threw himself on the throat of the snake in front of them. Arnie filled the air with a cloud of cinnamon. The smell burned the snakes' sensitive eyes. William looked back to see Gordon stab his stinger toward three snakes. They retreated temporarily.

"Go!" Toothpick yelled. Priscilla and the Katydids hopped past the snake in front and narrowly missed the ceiling. The fireflies along with William and April flew past the thrashing snake as it struggled to dislodge Swirl. Toothpick hobbled past rather quickly, followed by Paul, the roach doctor carrying the sugar ant in his arms. Arnie's cloud of cinnamon had apparently knocked Adam unconscious again. Soon, the insects were far down the burrow and saw daylight at the other end.

"We should go back!" William said.

Toothpick shook his head. "No. Gordon, Arnie, and Swirl did it to save us," the daddy long-leg said. "If we go back, it would be an insult to their memory."

"But what if they need our help?" Katy Katydid asked.

Priscilla shook her head sadly. "They don't need our help, Katy."

Everyone remained silent as they climbed onto the far shore of the river.

CHAPTER 10

It took them few moments for their eyes to adjust to the sunlight. Standing on the shore of the river, the peaceful sound of water rolling gently over stones played a contrast in their minds to the events they had recently experienced. Priscilla asked for a moment of silence concerning the fate of their friends.

Not long after, they climbed the bank and surveyed their surroundings. Toothpick spoke first. "Well," he said, "we'd best find a place to sleep. The sun's going down."

"I agree," Priscilla said. "William and April, perhaps you could scout a spot for us?"

William looked at April, who nodded in reply to his unspoken thought. "Of course we'll look for a place to stay," he said.

The mayfly and the bee once more took to the air. They flew high above the grass until they spotted an old chocolate-milk carton. They both thought it seemed perfect. April stayed to prepare the carton while William flew back to inform the others.

William landed next to Priscilla. "We found a milk carton that would be perfect," he informed the band of insects. "Follow me!"

William walked with them to show the way, and in a little while, they saw the milk carton. "See?" William said. "There it is. Neat, huh?"

Toothpick nodded. "That's a great spot," he agreed.

April did not sit idly while she waited for the others. She had gathered some crumbs of bread and candy left over from a nearby picnic.

"Food!" William said. "My stomach's been grumbling for hours." The insects sat down to dinner.

William ate until he was full, then made a note of something peculiar. "April," he began, "why haven't you eaten anything?"

April seemed shy to tell him at first, but finally William coaxed a reply from her. She made him go outside so they could talk in private. Once away from the other insects, they sat on the ground. April took a deep breath. "I'm a mayfly, William," she said. "I can't eat food."

"But you have a mouth!" William protested.

"Yes," April agreed, "but it's only for breathing and talking. It isn't for eating."

William stood to his feet. "How can you survive if you don't eat?" he asked. April didn't reply. William sat back down as he realized what it meant.

"Mayflies only live for one day." April said. "This is almost the end of mine."

"One day!" William exclaimed. "But, that isn't enough time to do anything!"

How much time is enough, William?" April asked. "For a mayfly, one day is like a lifetime. I've found new friends, helped them survive dangers. I even found a new family who loved me and I've loved back.

"Once, when I was about twelve years old in bee years, I fell in love with a handsome young man. Now, I'm near the end of my life. Even though I didn't do what a mayfly is supposed to do, I've lived a life more rewarding than I ever dreamed I could. I don't believe any other mayfly has spent a day quite so fulfilling."

William held the tears back when he realized he'd never see Swirl, Gordon, or Arnie again. He couldn't stand to lose another insect he loved. Despite himself, tears welled in his eyes. "Don't go, April!" he begged. "I love you! I can't stand to lose anybody else."

April bent over and kissed William on the head. "I won't go then, William," she softly assured. "I'll stay with you forever. Whenever you want me, I'll be right there in your heart."

She gave William a long hug. William did not want to let go, but she pushed him back and smiled kindly. "Goodbye, William," she said. "I'll never forget you." Then, she flew away into the twilight as stars twinkled slowly to life.

William stood outside for a long time as he watched the sky darken. He waited and hoped April would return, but she did not.

Priscilla came outside to check on the pair to find William alone and thoughtful. "What is wrong, William?" she asked. "Where is April?"

William gave a sullen shrug. "She's gone," he said. "She said she wouldn't be back."

Priscilla put her arm around William's shoulder and watched the moon with him. "I knew she would," she admitted. "She was a mayfly."

"Why didn't you warn me?" William asked.

"Because," Priscilla began, "some things are better discovered than informed of. If I'd told before what was going to happen, do you think you would have been more prepared?"

William thought for a moment. "No, I suppose not," he said.

"You can never prepare yourself for loss," Priscilla said, "because you won't know what you're losing until it's not there anymore."

"Why do I have to lose anybody?" William asked.

"To love another is to risk losing their presence," the praying mantis replied. "When you love someone, you find after they're gone that you can never lose that love."

"What if you stop loving someone?" the young bee pressed.

Priscilla shook her head. "You never stop loving someone." She sighed deeply. "I lost my husband once, but I never stopped loving him."

"I am sorry," William said. "I didn't know you'd lost

your husband, but you shouldn't blame yourself. It's just that...that it wasn't long enough. To know April, I mean."

"Love doesn't need to last more than a moment. An eternity rests in the small nutshell of an instant," she said.

William didn't quite understand what Priscilla meant, but he felt better for it. He had another question for the praying mantis, "Do you believe April has gone to somewhere better?"

Priscilla nodded. "Yes. I don't know if she has, though. To believe is to not know if what you wish to be real is real."

"You are confusing me," William protested lightly.

"What I do know about life is confusing," Priscilla admitted. "We should live our lives reflecting what we hope the world to come will be. We should live our lives to make this world a better world by our being here. If we're not better people for being here, nothing we've done matters."

William nodded. "You're right," he agreed. "That's why we have to stop the invasion of the beehive, isn't it?"

Priscilla nodded, and she stood with William watching the stars late into the night.

Kevin Noel Olson

CHAPTER 11

"Wake up, William!" Toothpick's gravelly voice said as the daddy long-leg shook the bee with his wooden leg. William looked groggily at Toothpick, and the spider repeated, "Time to get up! Breakfast is ready."

William rubbed his eyes and looked about the milk carton. The other insects already ate from the pile of crumbs April had gathered just yesterday. William went over and joined them.

Cindy engaged in table conversation. "Last night, I had a dream I'd become a beautiful butterfly who dreamed she was human. When I woke up this morning, it disappointed me to know that I wasn't either a butterfly or a human."

"I was human once!" Dr. Roche informed.

William did not believe him, and told the doctor so. "I don' believe you!" he said.

Dr. Roche shrugged. "Neither did my family when I told them I was a roach."

"Are you sure that isn't a story?" Priscilla asked. "I seem to remember Albert relaying a story like that."

Dr. Roche fell silent while he tried to remember if it were a story or his own life. "No," he said after a while, "I was a human once. I remember it clearly. Horrid business, that was!"

After the pleasant breakfast, the insects left their temporary home and traveled in the direction of the sugar ants' hill. William thought he had seen it before, and began to recognize his surroundings.

Although Adam the sugar ant belonged to the hill they sought, he appeared to have no recollection of its location. At least, he didn't tell anyone if he did know. When questioned, he'd spout off a long series of numbers followed by his name. Nobody pressed him any further.

As they traveled across a barren field of hard, yellow dirt, Sally Katydid pointed across the landscape. "Look!" she exclaimed. "What's that?"

The other insects looked as requested. A good way off a thin, black line moved across the field. "Maybe it's another snake," suggested Katy Katydid.

Toothpick shook his head. "No. There's no snake that thin," he assured.

"Plus, it's separated in sections," Doctor Roche pointed out. "It's not just one animal."

The insects decided to investigate further. As they approached, they could discern a train of tiny insects. When they were nearly there, Adam began to run towards the line. "Manny!" he shouted to the line. "Tim! Fran! Beauregard!"

William took to the air to keep up with the frantically running sugar ant. "Do you know these people?" he yelled to Adam.

"Know them?" Adam said. "We're all vacuunauts!"

Although the sugar ants gathered around Adam and gibbered incoherently, William felt it safe to land as the other insects approached. Once the noise of greeting each other died down, Adam introduced the other insects to the vacuunauts.

When Adam finished his introductions, William explained to the vacuunauts why they needed to find the sugar ant hill and negotiate a peace treaty with the queen for the bees.

"If you can find the hill," Tim the sugar ant said, "we'll follow you there."

"Can't you show us where it is?" William asked.

All the sugar ants shook their heads. "We don't know where it is," Tim replied.

"You see," Adam began an explanation, "sugar ants have a terrible sense of direction. If they are walking in a line with other sugar ants, they can just follow the line in the direction opposite and it will eventually lead them back to the hill. All of the vacuunauts have been living in vacuums, so there is no line for them to follow back. I thought all the previous vacuunauts were gone, but they were just lost without a line to follow back to the hill. This line was started by a few vacuunauts that found each other, and it keeps growing; but it doesn't lead anywhere if you follow it either direction."

"Maybe we can help you," William said. "I kind of remember seeing the hill. I think if your line follows us, we'll get there fairly soon."

The vacuunauts discussed amongst themselves, and eventually agreed that following William and the other insects seemed a better course of action than continuing in an unknown direction. Soon, the small band of insects grew by a train consisting of four dozen sugar ants.

The insects began their long walk across the field. They walked for hours across the grass, until William stopped and pointed across the field.

"There!" he exclaimed. "Do you recognize that boulder?" he asked Adam.

Adam peered at the large, grey boulder for a long time. Finally, he shook his head. "No," he said. "Should I?"

William nodded. "On the other side of that boulder is your anthill!" he said.

The ants became excited. "Really?" Adam asked.

"Yes! I recognize it," William replied.

"Well," Adam said, putting his hands on his hips and looking toward the boulder, "we'd better hurry, hadn't we?"

With that, Adam started to run across the field with the train of sugar ants in tow. The other insects took on a more leisurely, but still brisk, pace. In moments, they'd passed the boulder and stood at the entrance to the anthill.

"Where is everybody?" Adam asked, looking around. "There aren't any ants working! Usually, there are hundreds."

"Maybe they're on holiday," Toothpick suggested.

"Ants don't take holidays," Adam objected. "Ants work every day, but there aren't any here!"

"Well," William said, "we might as well investigate the hill."

"You can get into that tiny hole," Priscilla said, "but it's too small for some of us."

William examined the roach, the praying mantis, and the daddy long-legs spider. Priscilla was right; the hole was too small for any of them. Even the Katydid twins wouldn't fit down the hole. Only William, Cindy Caterpillar, the sugar ants, and the fireflies would fit. He nodded. "I guess I'll have to take Cindy and Adam," he decided. "That will be it."

"What about us?" protested Tim the sugar ant. "This is our home!"

"Yes," William nodded, "but it may not be safe for any insect. There's some reason for the absence of the ants, and it may be a deadly one." He shook his head. "No need for everyone to be endangered. I trust Adam and Cindy, and I need to find my brother. The fireflies will have to come with for light, but everyone else will stay."

"I don't know if I can let you go," Priscilla said. "It's awfully dangerous, and you're very young. You might need an adult."

William shook his head. "You can't make it inside, and I must go in." He turned to Adam and asked, "How old are you, Adam?"

"I'm an adult," the ant answered, "if that's what you needed to know. Plus, I know this anthill better than anyone."

William nodded. "Adam will be the adult," he said to Priscilla.

"Very well," the praying mantis replied, "but be careful!"

William smiled encouragingly to the insect audience. Then, he turned to walk into the darkness of the anthill. Adam, Cindy, and the fireflies followed him. The fireflies walked last so the light would show forward instead of in the insects' eyes. Soon they all descended cautiously into the unknown depths.

Kevin Noel Olson

CHAPTER 12

Even with the dim glow of the fireflies to light the way, the narrow passages of the sugar anthill felt unusually quiet. Adam, being in his own home, led the way with surety of purpose.

"Where are we going?" William asked.

"We're going to see the queen," Adam said. "She'll be the one to talk to about releasing your brother, and about negotiating an end to the war." The sugar ant turned another corner as he said this, leading them down yet another narrow passage.

William noted in his mind that he had become hopelessly lost, and at the mercy of Adam's ability to lead them out again. He found himself trusting Adam implicitly, although he had no real reason to trust the ant at all.

The turned corners grew in number while the darkened corridors never remained the same size. The light from the fireflies dimmed even more as they became hungry. The anthill seemed completely devoid of any other creatures; ants or otherwise. Finally, the group entered a room with a rounded, oblong shape somewhat similar to the inside of an eggshell. The room seemed made of some sort of ivory-colored rock. Two large, round holes stood at the other end.

"Where are we?" Cindy asked.

"In the antechamber before the queen's apartment," Adam answered. He pointed to one of the holes on the other end, "We enter through there."

William stepped in front of Adam and walked toward the hole. The fireflies followed, and soon the bee was looking into the queen's apartment.

The enormity of the room struck William at once. A large opening the size of a gopher-hole rested in the ceiling and allowed sunlight to enter. The sunlight waned as the room sloped downward, and eventually disappeared. William could not see the floor from his vantage point.

What the insects could see beneath included a row of circular steps directly below them. The steps were the same ivory-colored material as the antechamber. Areas of dirt separated the evenly spaced stairs. The steps disappeared into a sloping, dirt floor far below. After that, the light disappeared as well.

"Whew!" Cindy whistled, having stepped up next to William. "That's big!"

William nodded. "It's enormous!" he agreed. "I could fly in here easily, but I could get lost maneuvering in the darkness below!"

"Well," Cindy shrugged, "I suppose you'll just have to walk down with the rest of us."

"Yes," William agreed. The entire room felt scary and intimidating, but he breathed deeply and began down the strange stairway. The other insects followed him now, including Adam who had previously led the way.

Once down the stairway a bit, William looked back at the door from the antechamber. He shivered as he recognized a face, with the eye-sockets being the entrance to the apartment. With the mouth half-buried in the dirt, the teeth of the bottom jaw made a short fence that stuck out from the ground.

William shuddered as he recognized the object as a buried human skeleton. He had seen one once before while flying past the medical college. The stairs were merely the ribcage, exposed from the dirt that buried it.

He continued downward past the last rib to where a row of round steps made of shiny, yellow metal and sporting a man's face continued the path.

"What are these?" William asked.

"Steps," Adam replied.

William shook his head, "No," he said, "I think they are gold coins. People use them for money."

"I don't know," Adam admitted, "but ants use them for steps."

William didn't pursue the issue further, but continued downward with the insects still following. The gloom grew with each step downward. The light became little more than a dimmed memory here. Soon, they came across an enormous pile of various food-crumbs resting against a long, wooden plank.

"What's this?" William asked.

"It's the queen's food," Adam said. "She eats quite a lot, you know."

"Where is she now?"

"Over there," Adam said, pointing along the plank of wood. "Can't you see her?"

William looked along the plank's length, and peered to see a small glint reflect off a shiny object. "Is that her?"

"Yes," Adam answered.

The insects walked toward the glint. As they neared, the sparkle intensified. It soon became clear that the light reflected off a crown. "Your majesty," Adam said reverently as they approached, "I have brought friends to speak with you."

William said nothing until he could see the queen. Through the gloom, the shiny object became clear first. He could see it was a silver circular band with a large diamond as the object reflecting the dim light of the sun.

As the group neared, they saw the large, black, oval-shaped eyes beneath. They saw the elongated face, and behind the face, an enormous, long, winged body with powerful hind legs.

"You are not an ant!" William accused without thinking. "You are a grasshopper!"

Adam ran forward and bowed deeply. "Your majesty," he apologized, "my friend has never seen a queen ant before! He would not know what the queen looks like."

"No," William admitted, "but I've seen a grasshopper

before!"

A deep, masculine voice boomed from beneath the crown, "You are not completely mistaken, Bee. I am not just a grasshopper; I am a locust. A fine distinction, to be certain, but a distinction we locusts carry proudly."

Adam's expression turned from one of servitude to one of shock. "You are not the queen?"

The crown spun about as the locust shook its enormous head. "Am I the queen? No. I am a male locust, so a proper distinction would likely be king. It would still be proper that you call me 'majesty', however. Majesty King Loki, the locust-lord over the sugar ant hill and sagacious ruler for many years."

"What's sagacious?" Adam whispered to William.

"It means wise," William replied quietly.

Loki glowered at William and Adam for whispering, then continued; "You see, many winters ago, and by many I mean at least the last one, your queen turned me away in a time of need." With this, the locust wiped a tear from his eye. "I have one great love. That is the love of music. I was young, and spent the entire spring, summer, and fall playing my fiddle."

At this point, the grasshopper rubbed his back legs together to produce a sour note for illustration. All in the party cringed at the awful sound, but King Loki took no notice and continued his tale thusly, "At the time, I had become acquainted with the sugar ants, playing music at festivals. I had spoken with the queen on many occasions. She warned me to stock food and find shelter for the long winter.

"Having no idea what a winter meant, having never experienced one and with no interest to learn, I ignored her advice. It was that winter I nearly starved and froze to death."

"I'm not certain it's possible to die of two things at once," Cindy interjected.

Loki offered a threatening scowl, and then continued, "I asked for aid from the queen, but discovered, it having been a lean crop, the ants had been barely able to stockpile enough food for themselves.

"She could not offer me shelter, either. At the time, my super-size prohibited my entry into the hill. But, when spring arrived again, I had lost so much weight I was as skinny as a stick insect. Though food had become plentiful again, I vowed never to live through another winter as tough as the last.

"I walked into the ant hill at night, now being easily thin enough, and kidnapped the queen. I took her place as ruler of the sugar ants."

"How long have you ruled the ants?" William asked.

"For longer than any of the ants can remember," Loki replied. "That's at least a week, I suppose."

"We've never had a king," Adam objected. "You pretended to be the queen all this time!"

"Yes," the locust admitted, "you see, you sugar ants are particularly near-sighted. Since you were never allowed to approach the queen, you never got a good look at her, or me. My voice did not match the queen's, but since sugar ants are tone-deaf as well, it did not matter. I ordered the ants to stock-pile all the food you see here, and have been living like a king ever since."

"Did no-one suspect?" William asked.

King Loki nodded. "Yes, but they were disposed of quite easily. I sent the undesirables who did not yet suspect on missions as vacuunauts. As you know, vacuunauts never return."

"They have all returned!" Adam objected. "And once we tell them, your days are finished, Loki!"

Loki's eyes narrowed, and a dark grin overtook his face. "Who says you are going to tell them?"

The giant locust started to flap his wings, creating a strong wind. A great dust-storm rose about the massive chamber. The wind flung the insects away with violence as the enormous locust rose into the air like a helicopter.

"My army has been sent already to attack the beehive and they cannot be stopped!" Loki shouted above the roar. "I leave now to take command, and lead them to victory!"

With that, he flew out the hole in the chamber's ceiling. The wind left in his wake destabilized the roof, and large sections of dirt came crashing down on the insects, burying them beneath a pile of debris.

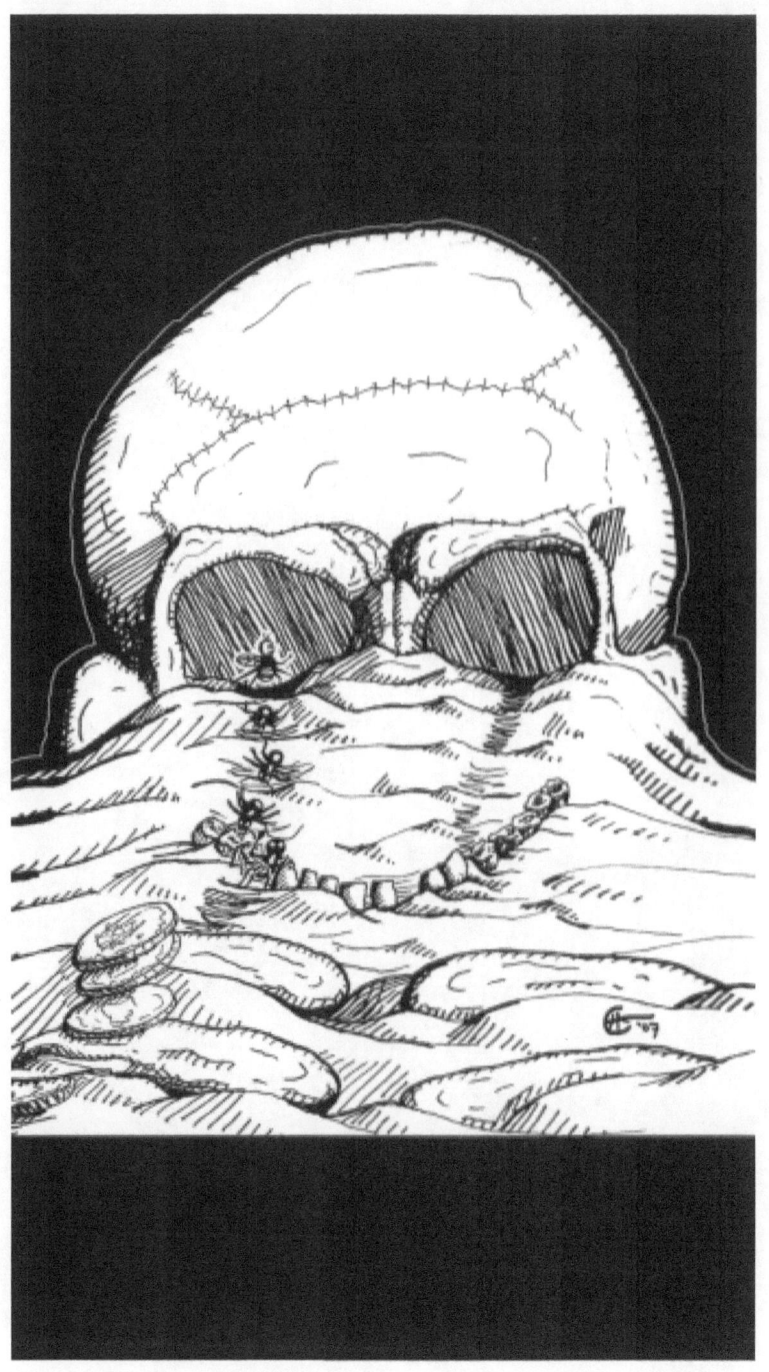

CHAPTER 13

William recovered from the shock of having the ceiling's crushing weight fall on top of him. He took stock of his condition and found, though he felt sore and bruised, he did not seem seriously hurt. He did not know how long he'd been unconscious. He could no see anything, and tried to wiggle his antennae. Like his arms and wings, he could not move them, either. The pressure felt unbearable. Still, the realization he had failed to find his brother, or even taken the time to ask Loki, and that the beehive may well be doomed seemed more crushing to him.

"Help!" he shouted, but this only rewarded him with a mouthful of dirt. His entombment had been total. If help were to come, it would have to find him.

He waited for what seemed like days. Finally, he felt the pressure on his chest increased slightly. Someone walked over him! The dirt didn't bury him as deeply as he thought.

"William!" a voice reached him through the dirt. "William, where are you?" He recognized the voice; it was Adam! William nearly laughed with joy. He had feared the dirt had buried all his companions.

He decided to make an effort so Adam might discover him. He used all the waning strength in his sore, tired muscles to try to disturb the dirt. He attempted to thrash about, but he remained solidly pinned. Still, even the slightest movement may lead to his discovery. He continued until completely exhausted. 'Did it work?' he wondered to himself.

"William!" Adam's muffled voice came from directly above. "I found you! One of your antennae is sticking out and wiggling. Hold on, I'll have you out in a jiffy."

William heard the sounds of digging. Soon, William saw light as Adam cleared the dirt away from the bee's face.

Adam's head came into view as William's eyes adjusted to the light. "Are you alright, William?" Adam asked.

"Yes," William replied. Truthfully, he felt weak, sore, and tired. Realizing his friends would rescue him, however, left him no desire to complain. "How are Cindy and the fireflies?" he asked as Adam continued digging.

Adam continued to dig in silence before answering. "I've dug everyone besides you out. The fireflies are fine," he said, "but Cindy's hurt."

William's heart sank. "How badly?"

"She can't move her legs," Adam informed.

William allowed Adam to continue digging in silence. Soon, he found he could move, and crawled out of the hole Adam had created. "Thank you, Adam," he said.

"You're welcome," the ant replied.

The pair rejoined the fireflies and Cindy by the wooden plank. The sunlight from the hole dimmed as blue twilight filled the room. The fireflies began to provide more of the light.

William looked at Cindy, who had tears in her eyes. Adam wrapped her in dried leaves to keep her warm. "Don't cry, Cindy," he said. "Everything will be okay."

"I can't move my legs," she sniffled. "That's not very good, when you have a few dozen of them."

William nodded. "I know. We can get out of here and get you to Dr. Roche."

"That's the other thing," Adam said. "The ante-chamber is clogged with dust. We have to dig our way out."

"We can fly out," William suggested.

Adam shook his head. "No. You and the fireflies can fly out. Cindy can't walk, and I can't fly."

"I can carry you out," William said.

"No you can't," Adam pointed out. "You're too weak right now, and Cindy and I are both too heavy for the fireflies. Besides," the ant said, "someone has to stay with Cindy."

William looked at the fireflies. Together they were

smaller than William. They could easily carry Adam out, but William understood what Adam meant to do. He nodded. "You'll stay here with Cindy," he said, "until we can come back."

"Don't come back!" Cindy objected. "You need to get to the beehive before Loki attacks and warn your people so they can defend themselves! Adam and I will be fine on our own." The caterpillar forced an unconvincing smile.

William knew Cindy meant what she said. He could fly up with some of Cindy's silk and pull her out of the hole, but only if she were willing. It would take valuable time in which many bees could die in battle. Yet again, William would have to leave a friend behind. He had no choice.

"You two stay here," he said as he forced back tears. "There is plenty of food for you. We will come back for you, I promise. I will take half of the fireflies, leaving the other three to give you light."

Darkness fell as William said goodbye to his friends. Following the light from the fireflies, he flew up and through the same hole the locust had exited.

They left the anthill at a place unlike the place they had entered. Tall, neatly-carved stones rested in rows between fields of manicured lawn. The full moon lit their way through the maze of standing rocks. The rocks had names and dates written on them, and William knew where they were. The stones were grave markers in the cemetery for humans.

Though William did not believe the stories about ghosts, he had never been in the graveyard at night. Long shadows of the trees eerily stretched dark fingers over the rows of graves. Sounds unlike those heard in the daytime wafted over the chilled night air. William shuddered at the creepy feelings, but he continued through the graveyard.

William attempted to get his bearings as through the darkness he flew. Suddenly, a flapping sound accompanied by a moan filled the air. William and the fireflies parted as an owl flew between them. The fireflies extinguished their lights and accompanied William in landing behind a headstone.

William noted how closely the owl had past. It could have eaten any one of them! Now, William felt scared for a reason.

High-pitched shrieks filled the air as a wave of bats flew overhead. William knew flying would not be a good thing with bats about. They would home in on anything flying by listening for the echoes made when their shrieks bounced off them! William knew the fireflies couldn't use their lights, either. Owls would hone in on them easier. He had to discover a way out of the cemetery, on foot and using only the moonlight.

He couldn't ask the fireflies for any ideas, because they didn't speak. They only communicated by blinking their lights, and that was too dangerous. William felt more alone than ever in his life. Which way should they go?

He knew where the cemetery was in relation to the anthill and his beehive, but not how to move in that direction from the inside. His sense of direction had been lost when he had moved through the tunnels, and he had no idea which way was which.

He almost laughed with delight when he remembered something. He covered his mouth to stifle the chuckle. He looked up at the moonlit headstone. The names on the stones always faced the direction of the anthill, and farther away, his beehive. When he saw the name 'Kirk Guard' on the stone, he knew which way to go.

He signaled the ants to follow him, and walked away from the stone in the direction the names pointed. He traveled toward the graveyard's fence, which now came into view.

Suddenly, a large glowing object rushed quickly across the ground in front of them. William and the fireflies broke out in a run.

Though exhausted and not prone to believing in ghosts, William still was not completely certain. Even if it were not a ghost, William had no interest in running into anything large in a cemetery. As they ran, William turned about to have a look. Indeed, something glowing chased them through the darkness!

CHAPTER 14

Though William could not make out what pursued them, he decided he and the fireflies must take to the air again. He shouted instructions to them, despite the danger of making any noise at all. William and three fireflies took to the air.

It had worked. Still not knowing what chased them, William soon realized it had given up as they flew over the cemetery fence. Once he could see the tall, iron gates in the fence, he could discern which direction to fly to get to the entrance of the anthill.

He flew in the direction, and soon, he heard something wonderful. The katydid twins were singing! The flying insects followed the beautiful music, and in a bit, saw the boulder.

The moonlight waned as the first rays of dawn swept over the ground. William felt tired. He knew his ordeal in the cemetery had taken all night, and daylight would allow them to continue right away. He could sleep later.

William and the fireflies landed next to the sisters and Priscilla waiting outside the anthill. "William!" Priscilla exclaimed as she rushed over to him. "You're alive!"

Ants emerged from the mouth of the anthill. Toothpick stood up from the tall grass. Dr. Roche woke up from his perch on top of the boulder and stretched his legs.

William nodded. "Yes," he agreed. "We are alive."

"Where's Cindy?" Sally Katydid asked. Speaking together with Sally, Katy did too.

Tim, the sugar ant also expressed his concerns. "Yes, and where's Adam?" he asked.

William had butterflies in his stomach. "We had to leave them in the anthill," he replied after a pause. "Cindy could not walk."

"You left her alone?" Toothpick growled deeply.

William shook his head. "No. Adam stayed with her."

"We have to go get them!" Katy demanded.

Priscilla broke in at this point, "There's no time. We can get them after we solve the problem at the beehive."

"Yes. In fact, Adam and Cindy demanded it be this way," William replied. "We will go back for them after we go to the beehive, I promise."

William went on to explain about how Loki pretended to be the queen and usurped her throne. After he finished his description of events, only one question remained. "Which way is the beehive?" Katy asked.

"That way," William said as he pointed out the direction.

The insects progressed quite a bit faster without Cindy to slow them down. Though caterpillars are nice, they aren't the fastest of all insects.

Priscilla and Toothpick's long legs allowed them to scoot quickly along while the Katydid twins kept pace with short but powerful hops. William took to the air at a leisurely pace (for a bee) so he did not outstrip the rest of the insects. The fireflies flew with him. The faster insects left the vacuunauts behind a little bit, always staying close enough so the ants could still see them.

The insect troupe made good time across the flat ground. They walked until late afternoon when William caught sight of a strange display.

In the distance, a lone bee flew with a series of ropes tied to its abdomen. These ropes in turn lead to the ground where several of the bright orange sugar ants held onto them.

"Robert!" William declared. He spoke to Priscilla on the ground below, "It's my brother! I've got to fly ahead and rescue him!"

Priscilla merely nodded in reply. William accepted the affirmation and sped up, making a beeline for Robert and his captors. They seemed to be moving very slowly, which partially accounted for William's and his companions' ability to have caught up with them in the first place.

The ants either did not notice or did not acknowledge William's presence as he flew up to his brother. "Robert!" he repeated.

Robert looked dazed as he turned toward the sound of the voice. "William?" he asked tenuously. Then again, "William? Is that you?"

William nodded. "Yes Robert! It's me, your older brother William!" William rushed forward and embraced Robert around the neck. "I was so worried!"

Robert returned the affectionate hug. "I missed you too," he replied. "I went looking for you. That's when the sugar ants captured me. They tied me to these ropes so I couldn't get away. It takes nine of them to hold me, though."

William released Robert from his embrace. "It's good to see you're okay!"

Robert's gaze followed the nine ropes that held him. "As well as can be expected, I suppose," he said without complaint.

William followed his brother's gaze. "Oh, yeah," William said. "We'll have to do something about that."

William thought for a moment. "Hang on!" he said finally. He flew down to about the center of the rope held by the last ant and grasped it. He then began to fly in short circles, spinning the rope around. This lifted the last ant off the ground. The rope spun faster and faster, until the ant finally let go from dizziness. It landed a good distance away. William repeated this maneuver with the new last ant, then again with the next new last ant.

He then grabbed the six remaining ropes and gathered them together all at once. This resulted in gathering the six remaining ants together. Four of them bumped their heads together and fell to the ground. The last two held on, but Robert re-enacted William's idea. He grabbed the pair of ropes and began to spin them about, and soon he likewise flung the pair of ants through the air.

"That's all of them," William said as he helped untie

the ropes from Robert. "Where are the rest of the ants?"

"They went on ahead," Robert replied. "They could move faster without me. They tried to force me to give them directions, but I wouldn't. They had to send lines of ants out in all directions until they found the beehive, and then start a line to the beehive."

"They don't have a line leading back to the anthill," William observed as he tossed the last rope to the ground. "How do they plan to get back there?"

"I don't think they're going to go back. I think they plan to conquer the beehive and stay there."

"They're going to have a hard time of it," William said. "It's going to be tough to defeat the beehive without being able to fly."

"Oh, they can fly," Robert informed. "They've captured a herd of horseflies, and have been training them for weeks. They have an entire Calvary and an Air Force to boot!"

William's face fell. "It's worse than I thought," he said. "With the horseflies and Loki, they could easily take over the beehive!"

"I know," Robert agreed. "We've got to warn the bees!"

At this point, the Katydid twins, the fireflies, and Priscilla caught up with William.

"These are my friends," William informed his little brother. "They are going to help us fight the ants." He pointed toward the advancing line of vacuunauts and said, "Those sugar ants are with us, too."

Robert nodded. "Good," he said, "we'll need all the help we can get!"

"There were more insects, but we lost them," William said sadly. Then, he looked at his brother. "Robert, you need to fly to the beehive as fast as you can and warn the bees."

"You could do it," Robert said.

William shook his head. "You have always flown faster than me. It is embarrassing to say, but it is true. Now is not the time to protect our egos. We have to do as much as we can to save the beehive from destruction."

William's younger brother knew the mission would require running the gauntlet through dangerous horseflies. He knew he might not make it. William knew this too. It grieved him to send his brother into danger, but it had to be done.

Robert said no more to William except, "I couldn't have a better brother." With that, he turned his face toward home and made a beeline for the hive.

"Yes, you could," William said under his breath. "You could have yourself for a brother."

He watched Robert fly away for a while. Then he flew down to speak to his companions. "Robert has gone to warn the beehive," he yelled as he neared them.

"Good," Toothpick said with a nod. "At least they can prepare, if it's not already too late."

Suddenly, the shadow of an enormous insect fell over the party. William's heart sank as he wondered what insect flew with such an enormous wingspan. 'Loki!' he thought to himself.

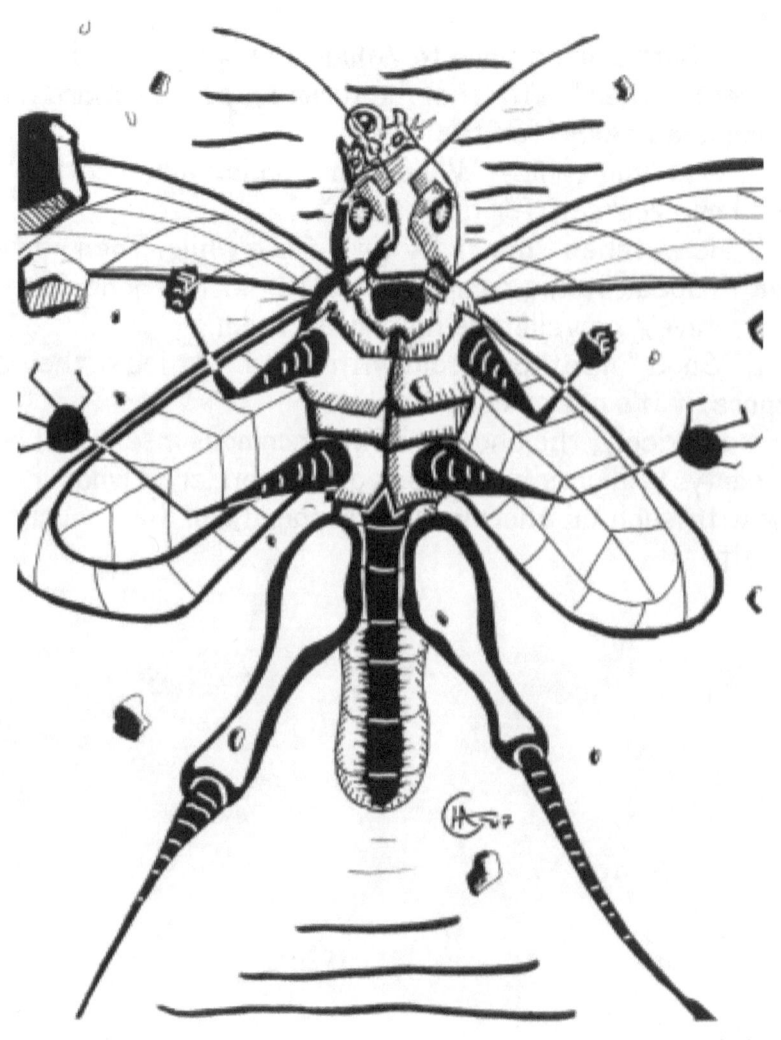

CHAPTER 15

All the insects looked up to see what made the long, stretching shadow of a flying insect. William was equally pleased and perplexed to find he had been mistaken. Though the sun behind made it difficult to see, the insects could tell it wasn't the Locust-King casting the shadow, but who was it?

The insect flew downward, and William could now see a large butterfly with beautiful blue wings. As it landed next to them and flapped its wings slowly, they all saw something rode on its back.

"Adam!" Toothpick exclaimed in a low rumble. "We are glad to see you!"

"How did you get out?" William asked. "And where did you find the butterfly?"

Before Adam could answer, the butterfly did. "William!" it said in a soothing voice. "Don't you recognize old friends?"

He had been so amazed with the insect's wings, he hadn't really looked at the butterfly's face. William looked closer at the butterfly, and drew in a deep breath. "Cindy?"

"Cassandra, if you please," the butterfly responded. "Cindy's a name for a cute caterpillar. Now, I'm a butterfly."

Adam nodded. "She cocooned after you left William," he said. "This morning, she broke out of her cocoon as a butterfly!"

Priscilla came forward, nearly in tears. "Oh, Cassandra," she said, "I've kept this thought in my heart for a long time. I'm so happy!"

Cassandra smiled. "Thank you. You don't know how free I feel!"

"You don't know how happy we are to see you!" the Katydids said together.

"I agree," William said. "We can celebrate later, though. We must get to the beehive and help out the bees!"

All the insects nodded in agreement. "We can't speed up the ants, though," Toothpick reminded. "They are moving as fast as they can!"

William nodded. "I know. We will have to let Adam lead them."

"Me?" Adam asked.

"Yes, you," William agreed. "Out of all the ants, you know the most about what's going on. If you follow the direction we are going right now, it will lead you right to the beehive."

"What if we get lost? Sugar ants have an awful sense of direction," Adam reminded.

Cassandra just shook her head. "You won't get lost, Adam," the butterfly assured. "After being without the ant-line for so long, you have begun to find your own direction. You figured out the path William had taken, didn't you?"

Adam's expression turned thoughtful. "Yes, I suppose I did!" He looked at William, "I remembered where I'd seen the beehive before, and headed in that direction!"

William put his hand on the ant's shoulder and smiled. "You've become a true vacuunaut. You'll do fine."

"I'll do better than fine!" Adam said. "I'll do my best!"

"No one could ask for any more," William said as he started to flap his wings. In moments, he, Cassandra, and the fireflies took to the air. "We will see you there!" the bee yelled back to Adam. Adam waved after the flying insects, then followed Toothpick and Priscilla along with the Katydid twins toward the beehive. A long train of sugar ants followed him.

Once William and Cassandra took to the air, they looked about the terrain. William peered in the direction they had been heading. With a little effort, he could make out the outline of the tree where the beehive hung. "Over there!" he said, pointing so Cassandra could follow. "That tree is the one with the beehive!"

William set a quick pace toward the tree. Cassandra

and the fireflies trailed behind the bee. They could not keep pace with William, but it didn't seem to matter since they could see their destination.

William flew by the familiar maple tree near the beehive. He was so excited he almost failed to look down at the tree. For the first time, he saw the sugar ant army.

The orange sugar ants had put the horseflies out to pasture eating the maple tree's sweet leaves while the ants gathered maple-sap dripping down its side.

William's heart sank as he saw the size of the sugar ant army. He estimated there were about 50 times as many sugar ants fighting against the beehive than there were vacuunauts. That would make about two-thousand, five-hundred sugar ants! About three-hundred horseflies buzzed around the tree.

William did not want the sugar ants to see him. It might alert them, precipitating the attack! He flew back to halt Cassandra and the fireflies.

"The sugar ant army is by the maple tree!" William whispered. "We need to warn the others before they walk right into a surprise!"

"Did you see Loki?" Cassandra asked.

William shook his head. "No. He might be preparing for the attack!"

"Of course, he is," Cassandra said. "You go on ahead. There's no reason for us both to go back. Just be careful!" With that, the butterfly turned around and flew back to warn the others. The fireflies followed her.

William turned back toward the beehive. He decided his best chance to avoid detection would be to fly high above the maple tree and come down when he got above the beehive.

William flapped his wings hard, slowly rising straight up into the air. The ground fell away as he moved higher. Once he thought he was high enough, he started to fly over the maple tree. He watched the tree, with its horseflies buzzing around the leaves.

Though slightly larger than William, at such a great height the horseflies looked like ants. He flew high above, always looking for any sign that the ants had spotted him. To his delight, he could see none. His gambit had paid off. The ants were too near-sighted to see him, and the horseflies would not care if they had.

William began his descent toward the tree with the beehive. He felt choked up as the beehive came in sight; he missed his parents very much! As he neared, his parents flew out to meet him.

His mother rushed over to William and wrapped her arms around him. "Oh William! We were afraid we'd never see you again!" she exclaimed as she nearly smothered him with kisses and squeezed him until he thought his eyes would bug-out. "We looked everywhere for you!"

"I know," William said. "Robert told me. I missed you all so much!"

His father wrapped his arms around both of them. "We missed you son!" he said with tears in his eyes. William had never seen his dad cry before. "We have both our boys back, Bee!" he said to his wife. (Her first name was Bee.)

"You mean you're not angry with me?" William said with trepidation.

"If you or your brother did anything to be angry about," his father said, "you've learned your lesson by now, I hope. If you haven't, being angry with you won't teach you anything new."

William felt relieved to hear this. "I have learned my lesson, father!" he assured. "Did Robert give you my message?"

His father nodded. "Your brother is talking to the queen right now. I think it would be best if you joined them. They'll need all the information they can get to defend the beehive."

William followed his parents into the hive post-haste. In no time, he stood next to his brother in front of the queen, with a pair of soldier-bees standing on either side. He had seen the queen several times, and he had always found her quite beautiful. William started to bow.

"No time for formalities," the queen said, gesturing William to stand again. "We've got to prepare for war."

William stood again. "Your majesty, the ants are at the maple-tree right now. They have about two thousand soldier ants, and three hundred ants mounted on horseflies."

The queen nodded. "That's quite an army," she said. "The bees ordinarily don't war with other insects, but the ants are attacking us. We must protect ourselves. Our army is only about five hundred bees, but if all the adult bees fight, we number around twelve hundred."

"There are reinforcements on the way," William said.

"How many?" the queen asked.

"There are fifty sugar ants on our side, two Katydids, a praying Mantis, a butterfly, a roach doctor, and a daddy long-leg spider."

"That's not very much for reinforcements," the queen said. "Still, I welcome any kind of aid. But will they be here in time?"

"They should be here soon," William said.

"Good," the queen said. "Thank you William and Robert, you are dismissed."

William and Robert walked into the hallway. They headed to rejoin their parents at home.

"Do you think we can help defend the hive?" Robert asked as they walked along.

William shook his head. "They won't allow us to fight. Only those who are old enough will fight."

"Mother and father won't let us fight, either," Robert said. "This is our home too, William! If we don't fight and the bees lose, we'll still be in a bad way!"

"I agree," William said with a nod. "The thing is; if we go home right now, our parents can stop us from fighting. If we wait until the battle, nobody will stop us!"

"We'll be defying our parents' wishes again," Robert

said.

"They would be proud of us, Robert," William said. "I didn't promise to stay out of the battle. I don't feel right about going against what mother and father want, but we need to help any way we can!"

Robert nodded. "Let's hide until the battle starts."

The brothers sneaked past the guards at the gate to the beehive and flew up into the tree leaves. They landed on a branch that offered them a wide view of the area. "Look!" William said as he pointed at a thin, moving orange line followed by some flying black specks. "Over there! That's the sugar ant army."

"Where are your friends?" Robert asked.

William shook his head. "I don't know. We might have to fight without their help."

CHAPTER 16

A beeline of soldiers flew out of the hive as the sugar ant army approached. About a hundred bees set several rows of large 'V' formations in the air. There were ten rows in total, with ten bees to each row. The horsefly brigade flew to meet them as the foot soldier sugar ants marched toward the base of the tree.

"I don't see Loki," William observed.

"Do you think he's spoken to them?" Robert asked.

William nodded. "I'm certain he has. He couldn't get too close, or they might see he's not their queen."

As they spoke, the first wave of bees raised a great buzzing sound and met the horsefly infantry. Most of the bees hesitated to sting the horseflies because they would lose their stingers and die. Instead, they punched at the horseflies. The horseflies, directed by the sugar ants riding them, bit into the bees with their powerful jaws and sent the first wave in retreat. Three of the bees fell, while the remainder went behind the lines with wounds.

The second row of bees took note of the earlier failures. The next wave of bees successfully used wing attacks to knock a few ants off their mounts. The dislodged ant pilots plunged to the ground below. However, the horseflies injured far more bees by their painful bite attacks, directed by the sugar ants.

Some of the bees fell from the sky with wounded or missing wings. Medical bees removed more wounded to the safety behind the lines to receive first aid. A hospital had been set up farther down the limb holding the beehive.

The third wave of bees rushed into battle. They knew what errors the earlier rows had met, and decided to take a more aggressive stance. Some used their stingers, jabbing them deeply into the horseflies. All those stabbed with the deadly blades of bee stingers fell from the sky to the ground. The bees usually fell with their victims, or right after. These bees had paid the ultimate sacrifice. Despite their brave actions, far more horseflies remained in the air than bees. At a one-to-one ratio, the bees would surely lose the air battle.

Meanwhile, the army of orange sugar ants reached the base of the tree and began to climb. A regiment of 100 angry bees flew to stave off the onslaught of 2,000 sugar ant soldiers. Most of the pilot-ants that lost their horseflies managed to fall with minimal injury to themselves, and walked over to join the foot soldiers.

"Should we join the battle?" Robert asked.

William shook his head. "We need to stay out until we are needed," he said. "If the other bees saw there were children at risk, they'd endanger themselves to protect us."

The brothers could only watch helplessly as the battle continued. The airborne bees faired poorly against the tiny sugar ants as they climbed the tree. The ants were too small to strike with their stingers. The bees had limited success buffeting the ants with their wings and using the wind they created to knock them off the tree. The only way they could be effective would be to land and attack them on the tree's surface. However, each bee that attempted this desperate act became instantly overwhelmed with large numbers of ants.

"I don't see how we can win," Robert said sadly.

William nodded, but said nothing in reply. Both felt helpless as the bee army suffered great losses of soldiers and ground.

The bees that fought the sugar ant foot soldiers discovered it worked best to concentrate their wind-power together and blow the ants off the tree. This proved more effective, but the onslaught continued.

The Bee Air Force had the same idea. They tried to blow ants off the horseflies. Undirected by a sugar ant pilot, the horseflies drifted away in boredom. This tactic became cumbersome, since ten bees might only be able to knock off one ant-pilot at a time. The mounted ants didn't congregate in one area as the soldier-ants did. If the ants held on, it became nearly impossible to dislodge them. The limited success the bees had fighting against the foot soldiers did not translate well against the horseflies.

"Look!" William exclaimed excitedly. "There are my friends!"

He pointed across the field, and sure enough, the rag-tag band of insects walked across the field, followed by the orange line of vacuunauts. He could see Cassandra flying in front and leading the group. The rest were mere dots on the ground from William's perspective.

"I hope they can help," Robert said.

"You would be amazed," William replied. "I've seen them accomplish incredible things."

On the bad news side, a string of foot soldiers had reached the tree limb holding the hive, and struggled slowly across. Once the ants got past the hive, they would likely proceed to the end of the branch where the medical bees had set up the infirmary for the wounded. Many of the horseflies now circled the hive itself, battling off the defending bees.

William and Robert flew high over the battle, and toward William's friends. As they approached the group, William noted some notable additions.

"Swirl!" he exclaimed as he flew closer. "Arnie!"

The spider and the stink-beetle walked with Toothpick. "Willy!" Swirl yelled as he waved.

William landed next to them. "Boy, am I glad to see you two! Where's Gordon?"

Swirl and Arnie looked at each other. "Well," Arnie began, "we got separated in the fight with the snakes. Swirl and I got our snakes, but one of the snakes went missing with Gordon. We didn't see what happened, but I don't think he made it."

"Oh," William said.

"We're holding out hope, though," Swirl interjected.

"Who is this?" William asked in way of changing an obviously uncomfortable subject. He indicated a sleek, orange-colored insect with shiny wings and attractive eyes.

"Oh!" Swirl said. "This is her majesty Queen Candice. She's the true queen of the sugar ants! Loki thought he had killed her, but she got away."

"Really?" William asked. "Maybe you could talk to them and stop the war!"

"I think it's too late for that," Candice said. "The sugar ants won't believe it's me after listening to Loki for so long. How goes the battle, by the way?"

William shook his head. "Not so well for the bees, I'm afraid," he admitted. "The sugar ants are fairing well, though."

"We need to find a way to stop the fighting!" Swirl said.

"We will probably have to fight to stop the fight," William said. "I know that violence is not the Entopian way, Swirl, but innocents will be hurt if we don't stop the battle. You will help, I hope?"

All the insects nodded. "Violence is always the last resort William," Swirl informed. "That does not mean we will stand aside to allow violence to occur to our friends. We will do whatever we can."

"Good!" William said. Adam and the vacuunauts arrived as he spoke. "Adam, you and the vacuunauts stay here. I have an idea! The rest of you keep going and do what you can when you get there!"

With that, William flew off. Robert followed his brother. "What are we doing, William?"

"We're going to talk to the Commander of the Bee Air Force!" the young bee replied.

The pair, not yet partaking in the fight, deftly moved through the aerial battle. They darted this way and that.

Nobody took any notice of them. Soon, they flew toward the Commander of the Air Force. He patiently stayed with the back row of bees waiting to go into battle. William and Robert flew right up to them.

"Sir," William said, "you have six rows of bees left. Across that field," he pointed with his finger, "there are four dozen sugar ants waiting to help us. If you let them ride on your backs, they can instruct your attacks better!"

The Commander didn't waste any time. "Great idea, boy! Troops, follow me!" he ordered. Prompted by his command, the last five rows of bees flew through the raging dogfights and toward the vacuunauts.

Like Robert and William before them, the horsefly-mounted ants ignored the non-combatants. They had plenty to handle already. The ant Air Force likely thought the bees were in retreat. That couldn't be further from the truth, but the ants wouldn't suppose any reinforcements might arrive.

William and Robert flew with the bees to make certain they found the vacuunauts. When they arrived, only the vacuunauts remained. The other insects had gone on ahead.

"Hello Adam!" William said as he approached the ants. "How have you been?"

Adam heard William's voice before he recognized his face. "William!" he exclaimed.

William landed next to the ant. "Climb aboard, Adam!" he said. "There are enough bees for everyone!"

Robert landed with all the other bees. They all took aboard vacuunauts. Tim had picked Robert to fly into battle with, and soon the bees rose into the air with the vacuunauts on their backs.

"Do you know how to fight off the back of a bee?" the bee Commander shouted to the vacuunauts.

"No," Adam admitted from William's back, "but we're vacuunauts. We are brave, smart, and an equal to any of those ants flying the horseflies!"

"Then let's roll!" the Commander shouted, and all fifty bees with their fifty vacuunauts on board rose into the air. The buzzing noise deafened William's ears until he grew accustomed. The fifty bees flew directly toward the furious air battle.

When the newly formed battalion of bees and vacuunauts entered the fray, the flavor of the air battle quickly changed. The vacuunauts proved fearless and skilled beyond the abilities of their pilot-ant counterparts. They hung off the edge of the bees, easily dislodging the ants from the horseflies.

The vacuunauts maneuvered the bees so the bees only had to worry about attacking with bites and wing-buffets. Though the vacuunauts were near-sighted, they made excellent pilots by picking out the shapes of the horseflies.

The tide of battle turned slowly to the hive's defenders. Soon, the remainder of ant-less bees regained their vigor and battled heartily. They distracted the horseflies while the mounted bees carried on their attacks. This proved extremely effective.

The battle thinned somewhat, which allowed William to see what occurred on the ground below. Swirl had wrapped a thick string of his spider-web around Cassandra and hung from it as she flew above the ants. She let him sink down into the ants and cover them with spider-web. She would then lift him into the air before the ants could attack him.

Before Cassandra joined the battle, she had flown the other insects to help at the infirmary. Arnie stood next to Queen Candice and Dr. Paul Roche while they helped nurse the wounded bees. The Katydid twins waited with Priscilla near the beehive. Their powerful kicks might prove part of the last defense against the ants.

William watched as the front line of defense broke. Ants streamed freely past the defending bees. They twisted Swirl unexpectedly as they passed and sent the spider into an uncontrollable spin. They rushed over the last guards defending the hive and easily avoided the kicks from the katydids and Priscilla. The ants streamed forward unstoppably right into the beehive.

CHAPTER 17

All seemed lost as the ants streamed into the beehive and toward the infirmary beyond. William veered out of the air battle; nearly knocking Adam off his seat in the process.

"What are you doing?" Adam demanded. "We can't run from the fight!"

"We've got to stop the foot soldiers!" William shouted in reply. He headed for where Cassandra and Swirl attempted to reconfigure their attack mode.

"Sounds like you have a plan!" Adam said to William.

"Yes," William agreed. "Remember what happened when you breathed Arnie's cinnamon air?"

"No," Adam admitted. "I don't remember anything."

"Exactly. The air knocked you unconscious," William reminded. He caught up with Cassandra and Swirl.

"Cassandra, drop Swirl down to grab onto Arnie!" William said. Cassandra gently lowered Swirl until the spider wrapped his legs around the stink-beetle. This surprised Arnie, who hadn't been paying attention, but he allowed Swirl to pick him up.

"Arnie, breathe your cinnamon breath on the ants!" William yelled. Arnie gave a thumbs-up to indicate he understood. William yelled instructions to Cassandra. "Flap your wings hard, so Arnie's breath spreads wide!" The butterfly nodded in agreement as she flew away. The strange trio of insects knew what to do.

The odd sight of a swirled spider hanging by webbing from the bottom of a large, blue butterfly and holding onto a stink-beetle gave the offending ants pause. The front-line halted in place as Arnie breathed his breath over them.

Cassandra's flapping wings sent the reddish-gold cloud across the branch and created a spectacular effect. Ants fell asleep and off the branch in long streams. Cassandra flew to the tree-trunk, while Arnie breathed again. Swirl directed the spray by twisting Arnie about as Cassandra created a downward breeze with her wings.

The resulting cloud inundated the ants still climbing. Some fell asleep peacefully in the nooks and crannies of the tree's bark; others merely dropped off the tree into deep slumber.

Cassandra returned to the beehive and dropped Arnie off at the hole in its top. He breathed into the large hole, and the reddish-gold vapors wafted through the windows of the hive. A few ants fell out, but most remained inside.

Ants covered the ground beneath the tree. They snored in unison and so loudly that the ground shook. The cloud affected only the sugar ants, so the bees and other insects moved about in it freely. A few ants remained awake, but they numbered in the tens rather than the hundreds and waved white pieces of cloth to indicate their surrender.

The mounted ants too, landed their horseflies and dismounted. After seeing Arnie's weapon of cinnamon breath, they admitted defeat. Not being vacuunauts, they knew they could not find their comrades to rejoin them if they tried to escape. They relinquished the reins to their mounts, and the horseflies flew into the air and away.

The battle ceased as quickly as it had begun. Dr. Paul Roche went down to tend to the wounded bees who had used their stingers. Many of the bees had lost them altogether and passed away. Priscilla consoled their relatives.

Bees wandered in and around the beehive and the tree gathering the sleeping ants and laying them comfortably on a nearby field of grass with the prisoners. The bees treated the prisoners kindly and fed them while their true and returning queen debriefed them on the details concerning Loki.

William stood on a branch, listening to the celebrations and wondering what happened to the locust. Suddenly, he saw a large insect flying straight for the beehive. He recognized Loki as he drew closer. The locust intended on destroying the beehive, and with his size, he could easily knock it off the branch. The locust would destroy the hive if they failed to stop him. William looked around for help, but all were engaged in tasks far away from where he stood.

William knew what he had to do. There were hundreds of bee and ant lives at stake, both inside the hive and on the ground below. He knew he would die if he stung Loki, but there was nothing for it. He swallowed hard and flapped his wings.

William flew straight for Loki, and Loki flew straight for the hive. Both traveled as fast as possible. William struck Loki in the chest before the locust reached the hive. The locust howled in pain as he and William plunged to the ground. Loki grasped William around the neck as the bee lost consciousness.

Priscilla turned to see William rushing at Loki. Swirl stood nearby and saw what happened too. "William!" he shouted. "Don't do it!" but William was too far away to hear.

Everyone turned at the sound of Swirl's voice just in time to see the impact. They watched the locust plunge to the ground with William. The pair crashed together. The two combatants disappeared from sight behind a knoll of grass.

For long moments, no one made a sound. Then, a sad strain of a note played out, and another as Katy Katydid joined her twin sister in a funerary song. All of William's friends and family wept for their departed loved one.

CHAPTER 18

It would be quite a while before anyone would feel strong enough to recover William's body, or even to observe the scene of his passing.

"He was a good bee," Swirl said to Priscilla.

The praying mantis shook her head. "He was a good spirit, and an example to all Entopians."

William's parents held tightly onto Robert as if they might never release their only remaining son. They thought they had lost both of their children at one point. To know they had lost William once again was too much to bear.

The insects watched the direction of the disaster. Finally, Toothpick grumbled, "It's not right for us to leave him out there like that. He's our friend."

Swirl nodded. "Everyone who wishes to help, follow us," he said. "Let's go recover William."

They began to walk toward the knoll, but a strange sight stopped their progress. A thin, whip-like scorpion's tail moved back and forth behind the knoll.

"Is that?" Priscilla asked.

"Yeah," Swirl nodded. "I think so."

They waited to see what would happen. The tail stopped moving for a moment, then began again. This time, it moved in the direction of the beehive. As Swirl and Priscilla suspected, the tail belonged to and remained attached to Gordon. The scorpion climbed over the knoll's summit, carrying the listless form of William in his arms. He headed directly toward Swirl.

As he approached, Gordon yelled to Swirl, "I found William!"

William's parents turned to see the scorpion carrying the young bee's loose body. They rushed out to walk with the scorpion.

Swirl's eyes filled with more tears. "Be careful with the body," he pleaded.

Gordon came close now. "What body?" he asked. "What are you talking about?"

"I mean William, of course!" Swirl replied.

"But he's not dead," Gordon said. "He's just been knocked out."

Priscilla, Toothpick, and Swirl all ran forward along with William's family. "Not dead!?" Swirl exclaimed. "Are you sure?"

Gordon shook his head. "I'm not a doctor, but he's breathing," he assured. "If you get Paul, he'll give you a better diagnosis."

One of the soldier bees ran off to retrieve Paul. In moments, the roach-doctor came to examine William as he lay on a bed of leaves. Dr. Paul moved around the young bee's body. He lifted William's arm and felt for a pulse. Finally, Paul put his hands on his hips and sighed. "The patient is not dead. He is merely unconscious."

A cheer went up from the audience. William's parents rushed the patient, but Dr. Paul held them back. "The patient needs to recover!" he demanded. "Arnie," he continued, "perhaps you will help bring the patient to consciousness? It's not good for him to sleep after he's been knocked out."

Arnie approached the still form and blew his cinnamon-breath on William. William coughed and became conscious to the amazement of many. "Where am I?" he said groggily.

His friends and family crowded around him, despite the doctor's objections. "You're at the beehive, William," Gordon replied.

"Gordon?" William blinked at the scorpion. "We thought you were dead!"

The scorpion nodded. "I tried to catch up to you in the graveyard, but I couldn't yell because of the owl. You flew away before I could catch up."

"You were the ghost?" William said. "You glowed in the dark!"

The scorpion laughed. "I guess I'm sort of a ghost, if you thought I was dead. I glow because I grew up in a uranium mine. If I spend much time in the bright sun, I glow in the dark the next night. It makes it tough to hunt. You're the ghost of the hour, though."

"What do you mean?"

"Everyone thought you were dead, William," his mom said as she grabbed him and hugged him tightly. "But you're alive!"

William understood. "I am alive!" he exclaimed. "How?"

"I didn't understand myself," his mother admitted without relinquishing her grip, "but I forgot to tell you about my dad."

"Grampa?" William asked. "What does he have to do with it?" His grandfather had passed away before William was born.

"Your mother's father was a hornet," his dad replied. "Your grandmother married him, even though she was a bee. They were your mother's parents. Hornets don't lose their stingers when they sting, son. You didn't lose your stinger, and it's not barbed. You must have inherited that from your mother's genes."

"You mean," William said, "I won't die if I sting something?"

"It would seem that way," Dr. Roche interrupted. "You have a stinger like a hornet, not like a bee."

"Yes," William's mother said as she held William at arms-length and looked into his eyes, "but you should still use your sting wisely."

William's father nodded. "Use it only in times of grave danger."

"I will," William said. "I promise." William had broken his promises before, but he made a vow to himself this time he would not break any more promises if possible. That vow he intended to keep. In the future, he planned to be true to everyone, especially himself.

CHAPTER 19

That night, the bees threw a big party. The day had been grueling, between the fight and the burials. Though it seemed rather early, the bees needed to celebrate their victory and the ants the return of their queen.

The queen ant had explained the events to the sugar ants, so they came to the party as well. Though some of the ants retained hard feelings against the bees over the battle, most were elated the war had ended. The sugar ants weren't naturally inclined to violence, only to following the orders of their queen.

The queen of the bees and the queen of the ants had already worked out a truce and a trade agreement. The ants would provide milk from their aphid ranch. The bees would supply honey. Queen Candice intended to make reparations to the ants Loki had captured the aphids from as well.

The bees had made quite a feast. There were honey-cakes in abundance, and honey-ale to drink. The sugar ants, who rarely relaxed, enjoyed the party to its fullest. The food, made of sweet honey, tasted quite well to a sugar ant's sweet tooth.

Toothpick sang while the Katydids played their legs as violins. William declined to sing in the band, but his brother Robert joined in to sing the 'B', 'B-sharp', and 'B-flat' notes. Robert could not sing an 'A' as William could, so the insects used selections that did not require that note.

The insects danced long into the night, all the while laughing and making new friends. William met his future wife that night. She was a beautiful bee whom he had never seen before. However, their wedding wasn't for a long, long time.

Priscilla had hurt her arm in the battle, so she sent William to get a glass of punch.

He looked at the girl standing next to the honey-punch

bowl. William's throat felt tight as he asked her name. He guessed it was the toughest thing he'd done in the past month, although he had gone through a lot since the shop-vac sucked him in.

"Letty," the girl replied.

"Letty?" William repeated. "That's a name I haven't heard before."

"It's short for Larissa," she explained.

"Larissa is another," He blushed and quickly said, "But I like it!"

She giggled a bit. "That's good, because I like it too. You're William, aren't you?"

William smiled and nodded. "Excuse me," he said. He turned his back to her so she couldn't see what he was doing, and reached into his pocket. He retrieved a small flower, but quite large for a bee. It did not seem too bad for the wear.

He turned and presented the flower to Letty. "Here," he said. "This flower is for you."

Her eyes brightened as they reflected the deep, blue petals. "Oh!" she exclaimed. "It's beautiful! Where did you get it?"

"It's a forget-me-not," William explained. "I found it in the shop-vac."

"Shop-vac?"

"I'll have to tell you my adventure sometime," William said. "It will take a bit of explanation."

"Thank you," she said. "It's the nicest gift I've ever received."

William smiled. He began to pour a glass of punch for Priscilla. "I'm sorry, but I need to take this to my friend," he said, "but I hope I will see you later?

Letty nodded. "Of course you will!"

William returned to where Priscilla stood. "So," the praying mantis said as William approached, "she was nice, wasn't she?"

William's face flushed. "You sent me over there to meet

her on purpose, didn't you?"

Priscilla shrugged. "Maybe," she said as she held up the cast on her left arm, "but I can't hold a punch glass and fill it at the same time. Besides, you liked her, didn't you?"

William looked toward the punch bowl where Letty stood. "I don't know yet," he said thoughtfully. "I need to think about it."

"Well, don't spend too much time thinking," Priscilla said as she took a drink of the punch William brought her. "There's only so much time we get to be happy. If we spend all our time thinking about it, we'd never get around to it."

"How do you find love, Priscilla?" William asked.

Priscilla gazed across the room. "Love's not something you discover, William. It's something waiting to be woken up inside of you."

"Like Entopia?" William asked.

"I certainly hope so," Priscilla nodded. "I hope the world wakes up one day and we will find a better way than fighting."

"You fought today," William said.

"There are some things worth fighting for," the praying mantis reminded. "To stand for justice and defend your friends makes it necessary when another would use violence for ill-gotten gains. Wars are won by violence; peace can only be won with love."

William nodded. He gazed back toward Letty, still standing by the punch bowl. "I do like her, Priscilla," he admitted. "How did you know I would?"

"I just took a chance," Priscilla said. "You never know if you don't take a chance. You should take a chance and go talk to her some more."

"I don't know," William said. "I'm a little frightened."

"How can you be scared? You just risked your life trying to save the hive! Now you don't want to risk embarrassment for a chance at happiness?"

William sighed. "I suppose you're right. It's not just that, though. I'm also too young."

Priscilla laughed. "You are too young for marriage, but who's talking about that? You're never too young to make a friend! When you've been friends long enough, you can think of other things."

William smiled. "I guess your right. I will go and talk to her!"

As he said this, Swirl and Gordon walked toward them. In the dimness of the moonlight, Gordon glowed slightly. "Are you ready, Priscilla?" he asked.

Priscilla looked sadly toward William. "Yes. Are the others ready to go?"

"Go!" William exclaimed. "Go where?"

Swirl walked over to William as the remainder of the Entopians approached. Doctor Paul Roche, Arnie the cinnamon-scented stinkbug, Cassandra the butterfly, Toothpick the daddy long-leg spider with a toothpick leg, the Katydid twins, and Adam the sugar ant vacuunaut. "We're going to start another Entopia, William," Swirl said. "You'll always be welcome to visit."

"Visit!" the bee exclaimed. "I want to go with you!"

Swirl shook his head. "No, William. You belong here, in your beehive with a family that loves you."

"Why don't you stay here and live with us?" William asked.

"Look at us!" Swirl swept his arm around to indicate the other Entopians. "A spider colored like a candy-cane, a scorpion that glows in the dark, a stinkbug that smells like cinnamon, and a daddy long-leg spider with a toothpick for a leg! We wouldn't fit in."

"It doesn't matter!" William protested. "The bees would love you just the same."

Priscilla nodded. "We know. We couldn't offer a major contribution to the beehive, however. We all want to do for ourselves and do for others. We couldn't do that here."

"But there's nothing wrong with you, Priscilla," William said. "You're still fine."

"There's nothing wrong with any of us," Gordon replied. "We're just different; we're not wrong. We don't belong at the beehive or the anthill, but we belong to the bees and ants as friends."

"What about you, Adam?" William asked the sugar ant. "You belong with the ants, don't you?"

Adam shook his head. "I've seen more than most ants, and there's more I want to see yet. I'm a natural vacuunaut, and I wouldn't be happy with the ants. You have a family, William. Now, so do I."

"I'm an Entopian too," William said.

"Yes you are," Priscilla replied. She pointed to his chest. "In your heart. Never forget that."

The Entopians said goodbye and moved, one by one, into the darkness. William stood there watching for a moment, as he held back his tears. Then, he turned and walked toward Letty, who still stood by the punch bowl.

www.ingramcontent.com/pod-product-compliance
Lightning Source LLC
Chambersburg PA
CBHW030524260626
47157CB00005B/1870